PEST MAIDEN

DILYS ROSE

PEST MAIDEN

DILYS ROSE

review

First published in 1999
by REVIEW
An imprint of Headline Book Publishing

10 9 8 7 6 5 4 3 2 1

ISBN 0 7472 7302 2

Typeset in 13 on 15pt Perpetua by
Palimpsest Book Production Limited
Polmont, Stirlingshire

Designed by Peter Ward

Printed and bound in Great Britain by
Clays Ltd, St Ives, plc.

Headline Book Publishing
A division of Hodder Headline PLC
338 Euston Road
London NW1 3BH

For Brian, again

Special thanks are due to the following people for information, support and patience: Robin Oliver, R. J. Perry, John Cash, Richard Smith, Caroline Graham, Alastair Duff, Brent Haywood, Ron Butlin, Regi Claire, Charles Walker, Mary-Anne Harrington and Geraldine Cooke. Any errors are my own. Thanks are also due to Hawthornden International Writers' Retreat for a fellowship in 1998 which greatly contributed towards the completion of this novel.

ONE

Birdsong, Dust, Delirium

Russell Fairley was unwell.

His symptoms: a head full of hot tar, needles in the eyes, ships' bells in the ears, nose streaming like a burst pipe. Every other part of him was limp; even his cock felt weak, sapped. And it didn't stop at the body: his brain, too, was stuffed up, congested with unwelcome and unhelpful inform- ation.

He had been hunched up at the table all morning, while the rubbish cart chugged and grunted along the road. He had sat through an orgy of road-drilling, a procession of loud, foul-mouthed school kids and the frenetic whine of a neighbour's washing machine spinning itself to orgasm. He had sipped from the same mug of coffee without minding the bitter chill of it. But on hearing that thin, intermittent squeak from the garden, like a rusty hinge, Russell's ailing concentration was knocked out yet again. He got out of bed, dumping his mug on the book he'd been reading. Cold coffee slopped over the rim and splashed the page; he eyed the mess he'd made with something like satisfaction.

The back green was bare and brittle; around its edge, shrivelled rosebuds drooped on their stalks. Beyond the iron railings, a car reversed into the cul-de-sac, turned and drove up the hill to the main road where, across a porridge-coloured panel of tenement, traffic slid in a sluggish stream. It was a drab, constricted view. Again he was assailed by that maddening, high-pitched squeak. This time, though, he identified the culprit. Directly beneath the window, a blackbird flexed its sharp yellow beak and drilled its monotonous song into the heavy winter day. It hopped a few steps and repeated itself. A blackbird. Birdsong. How in hell could birdsong be such an irritation? But these days everything irritated Russell. His entire life felt like an unscratchable itch, a rampant inflammation. He thumped on the window. The glass quivered. The blackbird flew off. His knuckles hurt.

The author has asserted his moral rights.
Moral rights? Taken a fucking liberty, more like.

He clutched the cracked spine of the splayed hardback book and glared at the coffee-stained passage. Every so often his eyes would light up with a pained gleam, he'd raise his pencil and swoop down on a page which already looked as if it had been attacked by birds.

For my mother, who won't like it
She's not the only one, pal.

This novel is a work of fiction. Names, characters, places and incidents are either the product of the author's imagination or used fictitiously and their resemblance, if any, to real-life counterparts is entirely coincidental.

That'll be right.

Of course *the author* had changed names, occupations and a few physical details but it was the kind of change, the cheap doctoring of fact, the sly shift of focus which scunnered him. Iona Rivers was fond of running her fingers through Rightman's '*thick, lustrous hair*' whereas Leslie Little possessed '*a naked, egg-shaped skull which didn't benefit from exposure; in summer it turned pink and peeled, in winter it was deathly pale and shiny* '. Russell tugged at a clump of stringy, unwashed hair. He was nowhere near bald. Yet. Thinning maybe, but who wasn't at the utterly unremarkable age of forty-one? Even Arlene – at thirty-three – had complained of hair fall, scrutinising her comb in horror and searching the chemist's shelves for products which promised bounce and body. Well, she'd found plenty of that kind of thing elsewhere – hadn't she? Anyway, baldness wasn't so bad, given the right shape of skull. Plenty of bald blokes did very well for themselves and some of the kids these days, girls and boys alike, regarded a shaved head as a fashion detail, even –God help them – an art form, though he'd never seen any of *them* sporting an egg-head.

And the names: the author, Franklin B. Fox, had rewritten himself as Guy Rightman, Arlene the Adulterous had been immortalised as Iona Rivers, while he, Russell Fairley, the wronged innocent limb of this particular pubic triangle, had been recast as Leslie fucking Little. No imagination was needed to work out that Little was a loser. Critics – and the book had already been given more than its fair share of coverage – had lapped up the alliterative possibilities and crude innuendo of the name: *Little Man Loses to Rightman*; *Little's Big Letdown*, and so on and so on. Why did Fox have to stack the odds so heavily on Rightman's side? Why did *he* need the winning personality, the interesting life and full head of hair, when he got the girl anyway?

From his grime-mottled reflection in the window it was clear to Russell that he didn't look his best: the five-day growth on his chin was more like a pot scourer than designer stubble. A frown had gouged a ragged furrow between his eyes. His hair twisted limply from his head like the overworked expletives inside it. His pyjamas gaped at the belly, exposing an embryonic paunch. He was on the short side and, as Arlene had informed him with enraging regularity, the extra pounds were more noticeable than they'd have been on someone bigger. If she didn't go for wee, cuddly men, if she preferred the steroid-enhanced hulks she no doubt tripped over at the gym, why hadn't she made a bit more effort to get what she wanted? But that was Arlene all over: act in haste, repent at leisure. Not that she'd done much in the way of repenting; not a thing, in fact. She'd just roared off to work one night with a bootload of her belongings, and hadn't come home.

'*. . . Between the worthies and the wannabes was a row of women, their staid office clothes jazzed up with ceramic pins and flimsy scarves in jade, fuschia, apricot. There was a muted, tamed look about them all, except for one . . .*'

Russell couldn't bring himself to re-read Fox's description of Guy Rightman clapping eyes on Iona Rivers. It was enough to make a complete stranger puke, never mind a recently dumped ex. All that '*pent-up desire he saw in her eyes*'. Surely even she must have squirmed at that. Grand notions like desire and the longings of the soul were not Arlene's cup of tea at all. Not the Arlene he knew. Waiting for the poxy little event to kick off, the Arlene he knew would have been bored and impatient, irritated by the delay, the poor quality of the wine, the uncomfortable seating, unflattering lighting, the lack of atmosphere. She would have been throwing together some scathing comments to bring home, like a carryout supper. Arlene would have scoffed at the very mention of desire. Until she met the author, that is.

'When Rightman came across a dissatisfied woman, he felt obliged, no more than that, responsible for discovering the nature of her secret dreams and giving himself over to making these dreams come true. Experience had taught him that women were like icebergs; most of the interesting material was deep under the surface. And over the years he'd developed what he liked to think of as his deep-sea diving skills, learned to read the surface contours and interpret them so accurately that when he plunged into those hidden depths, he would rarely resurface empty handed.

'Iona was a deep woman. Maybe the deepest yet; maybe the deepest of all those he'd had the fortune to encounter. But, like so many women, she had chosen her mate badly, a man with precious little imagination, a man who could only see her surface attractions and had no inkling of what lay below, a man who thought no further than a quick fuck on a Saturday night.'

Crap. Arlene worked too late at Boon's on a Saturday night to be the least bit interested in sex. Sunday lunchtime maybe, if she got her breakfast in bed. And deep: Arlene? Arlene was an open book. She'd tell anybody and everybody what was going on inside her mind – and her body – even when nobody wanted to know. There had been plenty of occasions – like the time she spent with Franklin B. Fox

– when Russell had wished she'd been a damn sight more reticent. So she wasn't satisfied. Some people never are but why should he take the blame? Dissatisfaction ran like a fault line through every aspect of Arlene's life.

She bought a book, a signed copy of the title Fox had been hawking on that occasion. *The Free Lunch*, it was called. It had nestled cosily beneath her pillow during the weeks before she moved out. Flattery first. Seduction second.

It was shortly after *meeting the author* that Arlene began having her hair styled and sorting her underwear into matching piles – even ironing it, for God's sake – instead of leaving a snake-pit of fankled tights and disintegrating knickers lurking in her top drawer. She joined a gym and began to spend money on clothes and cosmetics. She had always been erratic about her appearance, perverse even, tarting herself up when there was no call for it – or none that he'd been aware of – or slinging on some scruffy old rubbish on the rare occasions that they went out together.

With Arlene working nights and him working days, there hadn't been a great deal of opportunity but even when there was, their ideas of a good time rarely coincided. He enjoyed a meal out, something straightforward and sub-stantial, not the art on a plate Arlene served up these days. Or a busy, lively pub. Arlene despised the pubs he liked and, unless she was in the mood for checking out competi-tion, wanted to be as far as possible from the smell of food and hot on the scent of what she perceived as culture. When it came down to it, they'd never had much in common.

At first Russell had thought that Arlene's extra attention to herself was intended to please him, sucker that he was. He'd been flattered, vaguely excited. He'd even begun to take a bit more care over his own appearance and cut down on cheery nights in the pub in favour of boring, lonely nights in front of the telly, waiting for Arlene to drag herself home from Boon's.

Christ, he couldn't keep going over the same stuff again and again: he was never going to get any closer to why it happened. The only certainty was that it had happened. And every sodding bank clerk and night watchman, every rail commuter and golf widow, every bloody plant operator seduced by a squelchy title like *Eating Passionfruit in Bed* and a cover portraying a splatter of what looked like orange frog spawn, would soon know all about it. But the worst of it, the absolute sodding worst of it was that what folk would believe, no matter what he might say to the contrary, would be a mean, twisted version of the truth.

In spite of the low November sun shearing in, the room had a greyish tinge to it, a fuzz as if the definition between one object and another had disappeared. Over the weeks since Arlene had left, dust had settled slyly on every available surface, a powdery film on shelves and window ledges, a dirty fur on the walls, drifts of oose blowing across the floor. Arlene's absence was growing around him, a gritty absence. It couldn't be doing his respiratory tract any good but the vacuum cleaner was cumbersome and – from what he could remember – inefficient. The most sensible thing to do was go back to bed.

Foggy, mid-afternoon, half-light, everything drained down to pearly shades of grey . . . the curving concrete paths, withered thorn bushes, damp slippery tree trunks. The sun a weak, insipid disc, ghostly, without light or heat, just a hint, a reminder of what it might be at other, better times. There's that feeling about everything, the suggestion that this is not how things have to be, or would be all of the time but there's also a threat in the dampness, the clammy fingers of fog touching everything equally, touching and transforming, sucking out light and colour, contaminating everything with vagueness.

A warning, definitely a warning. Somewhere beyond the parameters of the scene, a red light is blinking insistently. Closer, on a dripping park bench, a man sits with his knees apart and head sunk between them. The man has his hands on his head and is tugging at his hair which is grey and tangled. As he tugs, hair comes off his head in handful after handful – like wool – until there's none left, until the skull is bald and shiny but he still keeps tugging at his head, pulling now at the earlobes. The head comes off in his hands and he lays it down on the path as if it has nothing whatsoever to do with the rest of him, as if it is something he just found there, a marbled, egg-shaped rock. No wound, no blood. A blackbird – its yellow beak alarmingly vivid – hops up to the head and begins pecking greedily at an ear. The body on the bench – and Russell knows this man is himself, a version of himself – gets up and walks away to another bench, leaving his head to the blackbird.

Sound. He's aware of sound where, before, there had only been vision; voices, children's voices, close by but small and shrill, a strange wintry chirping as if the thorn bushes hold flocks of children rather than sparrows. Laughter, high, chirpy laughter. The head unresponsive, inert. The blackbird still pecking at the ears, eyes, nose but the head remains intact. A stone head, now, a carved head, the eyes and mouth wide open, in surprise, wonder, horror, it's too hazy to tell. The blackbird, getting no response and no sustenance, hops on to the bald skull, fans its tail and squirts out three splashes of black and white shit. At this, the body on the other bench becomes agitated, fumbling in pockets, pulling out hanks of hair, throwing them into the air where they dissolve into the fog, the hands back in the pockets again, this time pulling out a coiled telephone cord attached to a receiver. Fingers poke buttons, a jingle chimes out, once, twice, three times, then a dead tone burns through the spongy, muffled air.

The telephone flies into the air. Sparks, flashes, fizzing: the telephone explodes quietly. The hands fold across the chest, the torso twists round, away from the wrecked telephone, the legs slide out from beneath the torso and walk away, keep walking, fading into the fog. Laughter again, deep, hollow, Twilight Zone *laughter, not from the bushes this time, but from the sky. Where a thin sun once glimmered, an eye now glares down at him, an intense, yellow eye pulsing above a mouth like a thundercloud.*

Russell woke with his teeth in the pillow. It was already dark. He could hear a ringing sound which could have come from inside his head or elsewhere. White worms of light twitched before his eyes, worms surrounded by thorny sputniks. He'd seen these before, under the microscope. God, the flu microbes weren't only attacking his respiratory tract, he was hallucinating the buggers as well. Car headlights swam across the bedroom ceiling in an oily hypnotic stream. The ringing tone continued. Maybe it was the phone, though it sounded faint, muffled. If it was, maybe it was Arlene. Did he want to speak to her? Did he want to speak to anybody? The ringing continued. He rolled out of bed and stumbled into the hall. Though he could hear nothing from the phone but a dead drone he continued holding the receiver until a crisp female voice cut in:

—Please replace the handset and try again. Please replace the handset . . . He did not feel up to attempting anything more complicated.

T W O

Pink Van

A battered pink van coughed to a halt at the bus stop. The passenger door swung open, scraping the ground.

—Get in, you dozy son of a bitch. I'm holding up the traffic for you.

It was Muriel Gulf, one of the lab technicians.

—Hurry, hurry. That bugger in the Rover will ram my backside if you don't get that door shut double quick time.

Russell climbed into the passenger seat and was immediately smothered by a mass of smelly, salivating fur.

—Down, Imelda, down down down! She won't bite. Just likes to lick. Men only, you know. Hates the smell of women. Except me, but only because I feed her. Dumb dog.

Muriel revved up, jolted forward towards the lights which were turning red and hiccupped across the intersection. The driver of the Rover leaned heavily on his horn.

—Dumb jerk, she said. He could have made it too.

—Perhaps he wanted to reach his destination without having to stop off for a blood transfusion.

—Huh . . . I said *down*, Imelda.

—Imelda? Fan of the wicked shoe queen, are you?

—Sure thing, Rusty. That's why I'm in your country and not my own. How come you're taking the bus?

—Oh, economy, social conscience, ecological correctness, that kind of thing.

—You think because I'm a teensy weensy Filipina that I'm a thicko too?

—I didn't say that.

—I guess I must be thick to pick up a creep like you.

—Look, thanks for the lift, okay? I'm not myself. Been off sick.

Muriel turned to stare intently at Russell, causing the van to swerve dangerously close to a knot of pedestrians on the kerb.

—You're still sick, she said. Eyes like dirty dishwater. Your girlfriend, doesn't she mop your brow and make hot soup for you?

Russell shook his head. Bedside manner had never been one of Arlene's strengths. And home cooking was almost unheard of, unless he made a meal. Leftovers from Boon's or takeaways had been Arlene's contribution to domestic nourishment.

Russell's symptoms: self-pity, self-righteousness, moral superiority

Muriel grinned. She had the widest grin Russell had ever seen. Her coral pink gums and even white teeth seemed to extend all the way to her jaw line. He wasn't sure whether this literal demonstration of grinning ear to ear was attractive or intimidating.

In the back, the dog began to whimper and throw herself around.

—Shut up or go to hell. Dumb dog.

Muriel took a hand off the steering wheel and grabbed lmelda's shaggy coat.

—Choccy drops when we get there, babylove, and not before. The dog seemed to get the message: it flopped down on the chewed, filthy blanket and drooled. The rush hour traffic had congealed into an impassable clot. There was nothing for it but to be patient, gaze at the window displays of kitchen ware, carpets and charity bric-a-brac. But Muriel didn't like being held up, even if everyone else was too. She nudged the van as close as she could to the car in front and hunched over the wheel, quivering like a compressed spring.

—How come you're taking the dog to work?

—She stays in the van.

—All day?

—I take her out during my breaks. She can't stay home all day by herself. She'd die of loneliness.

—Isn't there someone at home who could take her out?

—You really think I'm a thicko, don't you, Rusty? No, there's no one, okay? I live alone. Since my hubby pissed off. In the middle of nowhere.

—Sorry.

—What for sorry? He was a first-rate creep. He's gone. I hope for ever. I'm happy . . . Goddamn you to eternity on the City Bypass! Did you see that? Did you see that jerk jump lanes?

Muriel rolled down her window.

—Hey slug-head! You leave your brain in bed?

The floor of the pink van was strewn with slimy leaves and twigs. Twists of dried-up heather and an assortment of muddy pebbles slid around on top of the dashboard as they rollicked along. Though Russell's sense of smell was well below par, he could still detect the odours of dog, cigarettes and something soursweet like manure.

Holy Corner, The Sycomore Tree Café, Langue du Chat Fashions, Acorn Pet Centre, The Accessory Shop, Classic Interiors, The Gurkha Restaurant, Sea Breeze Fish Bar, the Merlin Pub, Safeways, Oxfam, Iceland, wine shop, pub, travel agent, the clock tower at the triple fork. Sandstone tenements, two-storey terraces, video shops, auto accessory suppliers, garages, bungalows – an outbreak of bungalows, an epidemic of them. *Neighbourhood Watch Area*.

—So Rusty, did you hear the news?

—I've heard nothing for a week but ringing in my ears. Good or bad?

—Depends. Whole place to be upgraded. Maybe even a rise for us coolies.

—Come on, Muriel. It's a skilled job you're doing.

—Bullshit. Your dumb country doesn't recognise my qualifications because, like me, they're foreign. To work at my level, I'd have to study the whole lot all over again and who can afford that? But it's a job. And I'm nobody's mother and – since my hubby pissed off – nobody's maid.

Water and Drainage Dept., slip road to City Bypass, The Steading, Hillend Ski Slope, Welcome to Midlothian, second triple fork, Damhead Holdings: Organic Products, brittle brown hedge, caravan site, monolithic Costco depot, TopMix, Robertson and Son, squat rows of drab post-war housing from which most of the plant operators and technicians were drawn. Hair We Are – Luxury

Sunbeds. The turn-off, the narrow, high-walled, windy road . . .

—Welcome back to Plasma Glen, boy.

The centre was an unremarkable low-rise concrete block. A couple of bulldozers were levelling off part of an adjacent field, in preparation for an extension intended to house, amongst other things, a new sterile unit.

—Just think of what those 'dozers might throw up.

—I'd rather not.

The irony of progress. Soil was the ideal, long-term incubator. Bacteria could lie undisturbed for centuries, possibly millennia, harmlessly dormant. Instead of past diseases being eradicated – medical press officers had always been overfond of that word – some of the nastiest micro-organisms had managed to survive in a kind of suspended animation for staggering periods of time. Live anthrax spores from seven hundred years ago had recently been discovered at the site of a mediaeval hospital. Turning over soil which had been left alone for any length of time was like lifting the lid off a pathogenic Pandora's box.

Mirrored windows on the ground floor and security cameras in the car park reinforced the specialised nature of the centre. In the early days, security had mainly been concerned with vandalism and petty theft. Blood products were valuable enough, though they weren't sold on the open market. Or even the black market. Yet. Though who knew how the relationship between product and consumer would develop, or between the plant and the transfusion service, the transfusion service and what remained of the hacked-off limbs of the health service? Whichever way it went, blood would always be a sensitive business and a measure of secrecy was acceptable procedure.

Muriel assaulted the brakes. The dog was thrown against

Russell's shoulder. She dribbled on to his jacket and blew her bad breath straight up his nose.

—Okay, babylove, you be good now.

Muriel tossed Imelda a handful of chocolate drops, blew the dog a kiss and locked up the van. Imelda rubbed her chocolatey muzzle against the windscreen, smearing it thickly with what Russell could only think of as germs.

THREE

Bloodwork

He could never get over the feeling of being incarcerated.
It wasn't just the place, though the shortage of windows
and the ever-present morgue smell of formaldehyde didn't
help. Maybe it was just the routine, the regulations, the
palaver of changing clothes. With the exception of management, who kept their suits on and didn't leave the corridors unless there was a serious problem, everyone had to
wear some kind of protective clothing.

Those who worked in the early stages of plasma
processing used the black to grey colour code, which
meant covering up their outdoor clothes in white overalls,
rubber boots, a hair net, face mask and safety glasses. The
human element was the chief cause of germs. Everything
else, even the air, could have its bugs zapped, steamed or
filtered out. So, for the sterile unit, additional protection
was required: seal-wrapped latex gloves, sterile suit,

footwear, helmets, the lot. The effect was a cross between an astronaut and a bee-keeper. You got used to recognising a person by their eyes or voice – usually raised to a yell above the constant screech and rumble of machinery – or by their gait or build. Otherwise, you read the name tag pinned to the unisex overalls.

Russell pulled on the blue jacket and trousers which marked him out as maintenance and got off down to the basement inferno where he had what was euphemistically called an office, a glass-fronted box off the main corridor with no privacy whatsoever and precious little sound-proofing against the racket. Basically it was a storeroom with a desk; half of the floor space was taken up with stacked gas canisters, steel pipes and other equipment. There were two memos on his desk: one from Todd, asking him to call in first thing, the other from Morris Morrison, the works doctor, reminding him that his annual check-up was overdue.

—Fairly bad were you, Fairley?

—Hellish, man. A walking bug bank.

—Well, we can't take any chances here, can we? Mustn't underestimate the viral genius of influenza. Just remember, back in 1918, that devious wee bastard killed off fifty million people.

—I can always count on you to cheer me up, Todd.

—An impressive toll, though, eh? We should take a lesson from the micro-organisms. Mutate and rule.

—Aye, well, they've been ruling me all right.

Flash as ever, in a dark suit and hand-stitched silk tie, Todd was running his chrome pen down the columns of a printout. It was what he spent most of his working hours doing, checking figures against figures. The man must see figures in his sleep, in duplicate and triplicate, the way everything had to be done here. As verification officer, Todd was responsible for ensuring that every piece of equipment was doing what it should do and doing what it said it was doing. Still in his early thirties, Todd was young enough to cope with being permanently busy but his workload was formidable. Russell didn't envy him his job.

—Hear about the outbreak of plague in India, Fairley?

—Bubonic plague?

—Pneumonic. Nasty but fast. It's been in all the papers.

—I haven't seen the papers.

Russell hadn't seen much of anything over the past week, other than his abused copy of *Eating Passionfruit in Bed*.

—Twenty-four hours and you're talking about a corpse, man, said Todd. Curable if it's detected quickly – tetracycline will do the trick – but in India? Think how long it can take to buy a bus ticket in India.

Russell had no idea about buying bus tickets in India. He had never been one for foreign holidays. The idea of trailing off to some hot, overpopulated country with dodgy drains and an unfathomable culture was too much like hard work. Arlene had dragged him round several European capitals in search of culinary trends and arty angles on interior design. She'd left him grumbling in chrome foyers and on glossy mezzanines, which had reminded him not at all pleasantly of the labs, while she scrutinised menus and seating layouts, lighting, crockery, cutlery, wine glasses, ashtrays. All he'd wanted was a cold beer in a cheap, basic bar. No, a couple of weeks up north, a bit of leisurely walking, a liberal sampling of the local pubs: that was Russell's idea of a holiday.

—I've only seen the airport, said Todd. That was enough. On my way home from Bangkok, the plane stopped in Delhi. We all had to get off and take our luggage through Indian customs before we were allowed to continue our journey. Four hours it took, four hours of shuffling around in the stinking heat. Wall-to-wall people in that shit-hole and a fuck of a lot of them were coughing. All it takes is one infected person to cough on you, man. And d'you know what else is on the up? Ebola. Flesh-eating horror story ebola. Not only that, humans are catching it from monkeys.

—This is a crap way to start the day.

—Just keeping you abreast of developments in the wonderful world of microbes. The Pest Maiden's on the prowl again.

Todd handed Russell a sheaf of printouts.

—Here you go, Fairley. Might as well pop up and see Morris before you make a start on this stuff. You still look like shit.

Todd was never ill. Prided himself on his lean frame and steely constitution, which he put down to lots of red meat and a weekly visit to one of the city's many massage parlours even though both of his restorative habits now carried a quantifiable risk.

As he passed the lab door, Russell glanced through its eye-level glass panel. Standing with her back to him, Muriel was pouring quantities of a clear solution into a row of test tubes. White coat, protective glasses, latex gloves, heavy black hair twisted into a knot. She worked quickly, her thin wrist flicking as she poured and stopped, poured and stopped. He could tell it was Muriel because she was half the size of everybody else in the room.

The clinic was tucked away on the top floor, at the end of the corridor, in the hushed, sanctimonious territory of the labs. This was where the brains holed up, and the brains, unlike other employees, needed peace and quiet to work. As the labs functioned both as a research department and watchdog for the processing plant, they were isolated – and not just in the physical sense – from other departments.

The works doctor was rattling away on his keyboard. Computer literacy was rapidly replacing bedside manner in the medical profession, which no doubt suited Morris Morrison, a pale, shy lad who wouldn't meet your eye if he could help it. Good-looking in a scrubbed, intense way – so some of the women said – bony cheeks, clear blue eyes and a boyish sweep of fair hair, of a type genetically predisposed to the white coat and dangling stethoscope. Replacing crusty old Charlie Forbes, who'd retired to the Italian Riviera to devote himself to sailing the Med for ever more, Morris was a recent addition to the centre, new blood, fresh off the medical school conveyor belt.

—So you're tip-top again?

—Better than I was. Couldn't slob around any longer.

—Fighting a fever can be the best thing. As long as you don't overdo it.

Morris ran through the usual tests with thermometer, stethoscope and blood pressure pump.

—Fine so far. Now, as you know, I need a small sample. It says on your records that you react badly to the sight of blood. Are you likely to faint?

—Not if I can help it, Morris.

Russell's reaction to blood was an irony which had made him the butt of more than enough jokes. In a year, the centre processed a hundred thousand gallons of blood plasma but you never saw red cells – unless an accident occurred and they were seeping out of a colleague. Plasma, which was the colour of thin urine, didn't bother him at all but whole blood was another story.

The playground, primary three. Micky Murphy calling him a wee shite for the millionth time, rage like a build-up of voltage leaping straight from his head to his fist, the crack of bone on bone, blood arcing from Micky's nose on to the tarmac. The brightness, the shocking contrast between the boy's pasty skin and the red gush where it had split. Micky had been stunned but impressed. Russell had passed out.

Everybody said he'd have to get used to it, grow out of it, in the way you were meant to grow out of just about everything – like talking with your mouth full, or lying in a cornfield for hours doing absolutely nothing. So much was expected of a child, so much whittled away in the name of growing up, so few compensations. But he hadn't grown out of it; the seed of fear had never shifted. Like a virus, it lay dormant, biding its time, harmless until the conditions were met.

It wasn't the idea of blood. He knew as well as anyone that animate life depended on blood's endless journeys through the body. He knew more than most people what its essential functions were and respected its efficiency and complexity, its ability to regenerate itself. The centre itself could take a lesson in organisation from its own source material. If blood were a multinational company, it would have a global monopoly in no time.

As a boy he'd watched plenty gory films on the black and white telly, seen black blood ooze and drip and flow, witnessed bootlegged banditos go down in pools of it, boys in battledress caked in the stuff defending to the end somebody else's patch, sharp-suited mafiosi blasting each other into yet another bloody cycle of retribution, velvet-cloaked vampires feasting on pale but astonishingly full-blooded maidens. He'd sat through all sorts of goodies and baddies shedding their black blood on screen and he'd been able to snigger at their hammy death throes like everybody else. But the real stuff, in colour . . .

—Haemophobia is more common among grown men than you might think.

—I just don't like it, right.

—Fine. So you don't do your bit for the donor service?

—Don't rub it in, Morris.

—Sorry.

—Look, just make some lively conversation so I won't notice when you stick the needle in.

Morris washed and dried his hands and worked his fingers into a pair of latex gloves. Russell looked out of the window. It was quiet in Morris' clinic, too quiet. He could hear too much, things he didn't want to hear; Morris sliding open a drawer, closing it again, unwrapping a sealed needle and tossing the plastic wrapping into the steel pedal-bin – this was one place you could rely on sterility – Morris moving closer, his dry, gloved hand brushing against Russell's too hot, rigid arm. His throat too, was hot and raw. Did he still have a fever? Morris hadn't commented on his temperature.

Through the window he could see Everett's white BMW purring round the bend in the driveway and passing the front entrance, which was reserved for senior management and official visitors. On the landscaped lozenge in the middle of the driveway, a gesture of welcome had been contrived: inside an eight-foot high reinforced glass structure which resembled an upturned test-tube, a life-sized Madonna moulded from blue epoxy and suspended in a clear, viscous liquid gazed heavenwards. At night the tube was lit from below and heat from the lamp caused the Madonna to rise to the top of the tube and bump her head against the glass until morning when the light went off. Very hot weather had a similar effect on the figure but as very hot weather was rare and visitors were only permitted during office hours, levitation was infrequently observed. Nobody was sure what the piece was meant to represent. Protection, purity, the triumph of knowledge over ignorance? Whatever uplifting symbolism the artist had in mind, there was something depressing about the blue lady bobbing about, forever trapped in a test-tube.

Everett's car sidled into its designated space, alongside the Saabs and Volvos, company cars for the top dogs. Blood was just another business, after all: the right people had to be impressed. Russell forced himself to concentrate on the car park where Everett was emerging from his vehicle, shiny shoes first, dark trouser legs wrapping around lanky shins, jacket flapping, one hand clutching a bulging, battered briefcase, the other setting the remote control for the car alarm which dangled on a chain around his neck. As he made his way to the entrance, the wind caught the tails of his coat and lashed them around his knees. Get on with it, Morris, get it over with . . .

—Well, Fairley, I must say, I'm very glad you're back.

—Don't think much of the patter, so far. Know any jokes?

—No, I mean, really, I was wondering what I would do about Saturday if you were still off sick . . . the do at your girlfriend's place . . .

Russell turned to Morris just in time to see the needle going in, the syringe depressed then retracted, the mls of his own whole blood rising darkly in the narrow glass tube . . . The room imploded. The chair dissolved. Black stars flashed in front of his eyes. It would pass, it always passed, just wait it out, think of something else, somewhere else, somewhere open, fresh air, good fresh country air, the hills, a scouring wind, a wide sky, swishing bracken, plump grouse, red stars, black, orange, red, he was losing it, sinking into blackness, his bones crumbling, skin shrivelling up like melted cling film . . . sinking . . . shrinking . . .

—All done. Wasn't so bad, was it?

Morris' voice eddied round him, a scummy froth of words. Morris' face swam in and out of focus. Morris' gloved hands rubbed an alcohol-soaked swab on his arm and pressed a plaster over the puncture.

—At nine, isn't it? I hate to be late.

—Nine, yes. Nine.

—Are you all right, Fairley? You don't look too good.

—I don't feel too bloody good either.

FOUR

A Defence of Veritas

Russell's symptoms: anxiety (oscillating), nonchalance (false)

Under the circumstances, he would have preferred a man. It was personal, after all, like dropping your trousers, although in this case it was others who had been doing most of that.

—Germaine Shuck. How can I help?

—I'm looking for some advice.

—That's what we're here for. This way please.

Ms Shuck strode down the carpeted corridor, trailing a wake of perfume. It was a brisk, authoritative scent. She was a tall, square-shouldered woman, in a tailored jacket and a long dark skirt with knife-edge pleats. Her bleached hair was twisted into a thick, heavy braid and secured by a black velvet bow. As she walked, the braid flopped fatly against her collar, like the docked tail of a horse.

—So what was it that you wanted advice about?

—Suing.

—Litigation? Against an individual or an organisation?

—An individual.

—Hmmm. So you have a grievance against an individual and you seek compensation for wrong done?

—That's it. Slander, libel, whatever you call it. Somebody's made an idiot out of me and I want to make him pay for it.

—Okay now, hold on, Mr Fairley. *Slander* is *verbal*. In other words, if somebody says something about you to other people that is offensive and untrue. *Libel* deals with the *written word*. However, neither slander nor libel are of any use to you here, Mr Fairley. They are part of English law. In Scotland the charge would have to be defamation of character.

—I don't care what you call it, I just want to sue the person responsible.

—Well, I don't want to put you off entirely, Mr Fairley, but it is a far from easy route to take and you wouldn't be eligible for Legal Aid. You would have to engage a solicitor privately and you could end up paying fairly hefty costs. I'm sure that if you've been reading the paper recently, you'll have seen for yourself just how ruinous the pursuit of legal action can be. I would think very carefully about it, if I were you.

Ms Shuck smiled briefly, a clean, well-balanced smile. Russell knew the case she was referring to, the latest fiasco in a long line of sex scandals involving politicians. But Fox wasn't a cabinet minister and nobody expected a novelist to uphold moral standards. On the contrary, novelists seemed to be encouraged to capitalise on their bad habits.

—So I'd need to go private?

—You would, Mr Fairley, if you decide that litigation is the path you wish to take. If you do decide to go ahead, we would be happy to represent you.

—So what do I do?

—In order to advise you, I need a few facts. Perhaps you could fill me in a little. There will be no charge for this preliminary consultation, Mr Fairley, in case you're worried about that.

—Right . . . thanks.

—If we decide to proceed then I would give you a breakdown on fees. I do feel it's better to keep clients informed from the outset. Our hourly rate is not what one might call negligible. So, Mr Fairley. Fire away.

—Well . . . somebody wrote about me. In a book.

—Really. What kind of book was this?

—It calls itself a novel.

—So you believe that you have become a character in somebody's novel?

—I know I have.

—How fascinating! I've always wished I were interesting enough for somebody to put into a story.

Ms Shuck frowned slightly and pressed her glossy lips together.

—Still, I suppose seeing ourselves as others see us might be somewhat unsettling.

—You can say that again. It's just . . . not fair.

—What isn't, Mr Fairley?

—Well, this book calls itself fiction but it isn't.

—Really.

—I mean fiction is supposed to be made up, isn't it? Well, it's not made up. It's true, not every single detail, but that's the point, some details have been changed to disguise the fact that it's true.

—Hmmm. And you're not too happy about this?

—You can say that again. Shouldn't ordinary, law-abiding citizens have a right to some control over what's written about them?

The phone rang. Ms Shuck transferred the call, smiled pleasantly, leaned forward on her elbows, tucked her hands tidily under her chin and looked interested but perplexed.

—I'm afraid you're losing me a little, Mr Fairley. To make any reasonable assessment of your case, we really need to get down to the nitty gritty, the nuts and bolts. In other words, what exactly has this author said about you?

Why hadn't it occurred to him that he would have to go into details, to draw attention to the very thing he wanted to get away from? How much was he going to have to spell out to this lady lawyer before she could even consider giving him any kind of assistance? And if he took things further, it wouldn't just be Germaine Shuck who'd want to hear about the bloody nuts and bolts.

Behind Ms Shuck's desk was an imposing marble fireplace, the kind which had been stolen so often that you saw signs in the windows of empty New Town properties which said: All fireplaces have been removed. Ms Shuck's mantelpiece held a collection of model dachshunds, from a small bronze sculpture to a velveteen bean bag toy. On the wall above the fireplace was a framed enlargement of three shiny-coated sausage dogs walking in a line. The personal touch.

—It's not like there's an individual incident – well there are plenty, too damn many – but it's not the incidents in themselves, it's what they add up to, the kind of person they add up to.

—Which is based on you?

—Which is me. There's a disclaimer, of course.

—Ah yes.

—Names are changed, a few other minor details, and I mean very minor, very trivial, superficial. Anybody would recognise me.

—So you're a celebrity yourself, Mr Fairley? Should I recognise you? If it's TV, forget it. I rarely find the time for the box.

—No, I'm nobody. Just an ordinary bloke. The author, well, he's not exactly a household name here – maybe he is in America – but what I'm saying is, he's taken my . . . he's taken me and put me in print and I'm not at all happy about it.

He should have gone to a smaller practice. These city centre firms were too big, too grand; intimidating. Too bloody well off. The oak panelling, brass fitments and plaster cornices were very tasteful, durable and conservative. Things as they were. Polish and preservation.

—Have you proof? That it's you, I mean. Would a friend, acquaintance or family member be able to stand up in court and say that this character . . .?

—Little. Leslie Little. The *author* doesn't veer too far from fact in his choice of name for me, does he?

—Oh dear. It doesn't sound very promising, does it? Leslie Little. Sorry. So, this fictional you. Would anyone be prepared to stand up in court and say that Mr Little is without a doubt Mr Fairley but not Mr Fairley as he really is? It is something of a tangled web, isn't it? But very interesting. We don't really do much of this kind of thing, and none through Legal Aid, as I said earlier. But you see, *Scots* Law is a very different thing from English or American Law.

—A law unto itself.

—That pun was amusing in the Middle Ages, Mr Fairley.

—I'm wasting your time.

—Not at all. No, it makes a change from the usual stuff about in-laws bad-mouthing an offspring's ex after marital breakdown. Is anyone else involved in all this, apart from yourself and the author? Male or female by the way?

—Male. And yes. My ex-girlfriend.

—Ahh. And what kind of press does she get?

—The works: up on a pedestal, flat out on the casting couch . . .

—Hmmm, I expect your feelings must be more than a little bruised. So your ex-girlfriend, who took up with *the author* – did these relations occur simultaneously or consecutively? It does make a difference, from a legal point of view, if not an emotional one.

—She was living with me, she met this writer. I found out about it a lot later. We had a fight. She moved out.

—With the author?

—No, just out.

The phone rang again. Ms Shuck glanced at her watch before transferring the call.

—I think I'm getting something of the picture. This *author* stole your girlfriend then capitalised on his crime, so to speak.

—Something like that.

—Well, it seems to me that what it might boil down to is whether – if you are in fact represented here as a charac-ter – you are represented *truly* or not. Because if you are represented truly you would, I'm afraid to say, be up against a defence of *veritas*. You see, if what this person is saying about you is true, what can you really complain about? That's the crux of it, Mr Fairley.

She paused, giving Russell time to recover from this unexpected blow. It was all right if it was true? How could it be all right? It was like saying spying was all right as long as the information was accurate.

—On top of *veritas*, there's the business of damage. There has to be some proof of damage. Did you in fact suffer what could be considered *damage* ? For example, did you suffer any loss of earnings? Did you experience any lasting physical or mental impairment?

Damage? He didn't have any broken bones, hadn't been bankrupted, wasn't on Prozac or Viagra — yet — but there was damage all right. Plenty. Though not the kind he could give a name to.

F I V E

Bloodlust

It had been nice enough when Russell had left town, parky but bright, but by the time the bus dropped him off, clouds had gathered on the ridge and the wind was already carrying a clammy mist down from the hills. Bloody country. Bloody miserable, unreliable country. It was not looking promising, not at all promising. Since Arlene and the car had left him, he hadn't got out to the hills at all and he'd been missing his walks: the sky, the springy turf, the peace and quiet, the views. He could forget about views for a start. The landscape was fading away, the coastline dissolving into a grey monotony, the city sights vanishing, spire by historic spire.

He marched briskly along the boundary between two very long, ploughed fields – a leisurely stroll was out of the question – crossed the stile and carried on to the foothills. The sheep were munching what little was left of the grass.

As he passed, they eyed him hopefully, as if he might have a couple of turnips stashed beneath his jacket. Their filthy coats were thick but beneath the clotted woollen dreadlocks they were scraggy, lethargic beasts.

He'd grown up around sheep, and remembered them as frisky, mischievous buggers which would trot along beside you, nudging you with their long snooty noses. When he was wee, one had bitten the arse right out of his shorts but he'd never held it against them. And, contrary to Franklin Fox's clichéd delusion about country boys, he'd never had the slightest urge to shag a sheep. Nor anything else on four legs. In adolescence, sex had been a predominantly solitary affair, an outdoor pursuit whenever possible, a communing with nature in sheltered, craggy nooks with the hills, the sky, the wheeling hawks and scurrying rodents for company. He had fantasised about girls he knew and girls he didn't and girls he could barely imagine, scattered his seed here, there and everywhere and nobody was ever any the wiser. Except maybe Ailsa Duggan.

Ailsa Duggan had frizzy orange hair, orange freckles, white skin and white eyelashes. She wore frilly dresses when all the other girls wore jeans or miniskirts, and lived with her granny and great-aunt in a crumbling house near the school, which had once been the manse. In fourth year, he and Alisa were in the same biology class. As equipment was limited, pupils worked in pairs for experiments. The teacher, Hector Stott, a tweedy, moustachioed beanpole who preferred pipe-smoking in the storeroom to teaching, had paired Russell with Ailsa. As there were nine boys and nine girls, Stott's decision was a matter of arithmetic rather than malice, though that didn't prevent an outbreak of smirks and sniggers and, towards the end of term, some illustrated toilet graffiti: *Duggan's Fairley Fucked*, *Duggan's a Fairley shag* and so on.

Because of the party dresses, Ailsa was generally regarded as weird, and, as such, was a bit of an outcast. She did, however, possess certain qualities which Russell – perhaps more than most people – came to appreciate. He'd known that biology involved some dissection but, through some loophole in his thinking, it hadn't occurred to him that there would be any actual blood to deal with. When Stott cheerfully handed out plastic bags containing livers, kidneys and eyeballs slopping around in formaldehyde and their own blood, Russell's stomach began to mutiny. When the pregnant rats, spreadeagled on wooden chopping blocks, began to be circulated, he thought he'd have to chuck biology, his best subject, before he chucked his school dinner all over the specimens. The gunmetal smell of blood blocked his nostrils, the roaring in his own veins blocked his ears . . .

—I can't wait to get stuck in.

Ailsa grinned. She prodded a squelchy bag of eyeballs with bony fingers. Her gums were pale grey, her teeth parsnip yellow, her sweat sweetish, oniony. He was saved. Alisa did all the cutting up. Without lifting his eyes from the report book, Russell took detailed notes from Ailsa's observations. They made such a good team that Stott awarded them the practical prize for the year. Ailsa was over the moon. She spent her book token on a luridly illustrated *Stiffs, Then and Now: A History of Dissection*.

—I've never won anything in my life, she told him. I'm obliged, Russell. I'm in your debt.

Though her elderly guardians had influenced her clothes and speech, Ailsa was otherwise left to her own devices. One sticky afternoon during the school holidays, she called round to the house and asked, coyly, to see his rock collection. Assuming – with a mixture of hope and dread – that this was a pretext for more intimate possibilities, he invited her in. His rock collection was just a tray of bits and pieces he'd found in the hills, a couple of chunks of fool's gold, tiger's eye, a dozen or so coloured quartz pebbles, an insignificant amethyst cluster and a finger's worth of haematite. Ailsa was polite but unimpressed by anything except the haematite and even that disappointed her by not looking a bit like the blood it was named after. After the rock viewing was over, she just stood in the middle of the hot, small room, humming tunelessly. Between them, a couple of flies copulated in mid-air. Ailsa giggled, blushed and looked at the ceiling. It occurred to Russell that, as he was alone in his bedroom with a girl, with nobody else in the house, he might as well find out whether her delight in dead, dismembered organs would extend to a living, throbbing, tumescent one. It could have been his clumsy attempt to kiss her neck and direct her bloodless fingers towards his fly or the sound of the front door opening and shutting which changed her mind so suddenly. Whatever, she broke free of him, overturning the tray of specimens as she fled from the room, leaving him to pick up his rock collection and quickly think up a lie about why that lass was in such a hurry to leave.

The low-lying mist was coiling around him and he couldn't see any sign of the path which led to the ridge. The mist might not be a serious problem but he could tell from the sky that the weather was unsettled. There were only a few hours of daylight left: three, four maybe at most. If he found the path soon, he'd probably be fine; he'd done the ridge walk often enough but anybody could get into difficulty in this kind of weather, if you lost sight of your landmarks and already he could barely see the hills. Bugger it.

Russell stood at the bus stop. And stood. And cursed Arlene's desertion. Her farewell note: *I can't run Boon's without wheels. There's an excellent bus service so you shouldn't have any problems.* No apologies, no consolatory platitudes, no sweetener on the bitter pill, no no, none of that slop. Just a fucking commentary on the quality of public transport. Which wasn't that bloody good. As for Arlene taking the car, he too had put time, money and labour into it. Something else to be sorted out: custody of the car.

SIX

Nice Price

Mrs Ramasawmy was perched on a packing box, reading the paper. A small, rounded woman, her stringy pony tail trailed down the back of a shapeless cardigan. She passed a weary hand over her brow.

—You read about this plague problem in Delhi? Very bad.

—Frightening, isn't it?

—Frightening, yeah, frightening. I have two sisters in Delhi. Seven nieces and nephews.

—Have you been in touch? Have you phoned?

—Tonight I try to phone but Panjit say all lines will be busy, I won't get connection. But I try tonight. After close up shop.

She tossed the paper on to a tray of onions and looked up.

—Your girlfriend, she's away on holidays?

—Just away. Gone.

She nodded. Her dark eyes filmed over with a warm, compassionate glaze. She rang up the total and gently placed the change in his hand instead of slapping it down on the counter, as she usually did. Her small kindness made him feel lonely.

As he turned the corner into his own street, a blur of gold and turquoise shimmered along the pavement towards him: Sonia and Parveen, on bicycles they'd long outgrown. He hopped sideways to dodge a collision with their spinning wheels. Their feathery laughter flew in his face.

—Where's Arlene?

—I don't know.

The girls were too far away to hear him add that he didn't care either.

Sonia and Parveen were Mrs Ramasawmy's daughters. They were decked out as usual in satin dresses and leggings, beads and bracelets, ribbons and shiny clasps. Other kids played out in the summer but this pair were out in all but the worst weather. Arlene had got to know them the previous year, when Nice Price opened up. They liked to show her their new gold slippers, earrings, jewelled nose studs, their fluorescent skipping ropes. Arlene would sit on the front step on sunny evenings when she wasn't working, fending off their questions: *How old are you? How old is your boyfriend? Why don't you have any babies yet?* and scanning mail order catalogues and prize-draw leaflets, fantasising about how her unsatisfactory existence would alter beyond all recognition if one of those dream homes or holidays of a lifetime promised by the daily deluge of junk mail had her name on it. Then she'd check the employment pages in the newspaper. Even though Boon's had gone from strength to strength, Arlene talked of chucking it every other week and the Sits. Vac. columns had been her favourite reading material. Before, that is, her own most intimate moments were available in print.

He'd never seen anyone read job descriptions with Arlene's enthusiasm and optimism. From beginning to end she'd read them, twice usually in case she missed a golden opportunity. It didn't matter how unlikely a candidate she was, she would consider just about everything, from abattoir assistant to church warden. *You've got to believe that some change is possible*: Arlene.

Russell had stopped believing in any change other than deterioration. He detested most things about his job but it was the best of its kind available to him. And that was all most people could really expect, wasn't it? Life was just a kind of processing plant. People came into the world whole complete beings with unlimited potential but the world had less and less need of whole individuals; only marketable extracts were required.

In the early days in his field of work, whole blood had been siphoned out of willing donors when only a fraction of its constituents was required. It was a hugely wasteful process and resulted in supply frequently falling short of demand. Since it had become possible to extract plasma from whole blood, many donors now had their cooled blood – minus the valuable plasma – returned to their veins. That's how he felt about his life; as if the valuable ingredients had been siphoned off for someone else's use, as if he'd been left with an inferior constitution. But most people must feel like that, most people's working lives didn't really add up to much, which was why they didn't spend more time than necessary thinking about their jobs. Weekends and holidays were what most people lived for –

time off. *Most people? Who are these most people?*: Arlene.

Before he'd reached the end of the street, the girls had turned their bikes and begun pedalling wildly towards him again. How much time off did their mother get? The hours she endured at the till of Nice Price, perching on an upturned box, ringing up sales, trying patiently to decipher the slurred speech of boozers who mooched in and out from early morning to late night, the labour involved in keeping her girls turned out like princesses.

Russell put his messages on the doorstep while he searched his pockets for his key. Across the road, the first-floor window was open and a sound system was belching out a demented, head-splitting racket. The lads who'd been unloading their van in the morning had clearly moved in and noisy bloody neighbours, Christ, he could do without them. Since Arlene had left him, he'd become sensitive to noise; sounds he'd never noticed before had begun to torment him, especially at night: the gas meter, the radiator, fridge, bathroom fan, all humming and clicking away with their own unfathomable patterns. But footsteps were the worst. He'd be lying on his long-unwashed sheets trying to sleep when he'd hear someone in the distance, tip tapping nearer and nearer. As the footsteps approached, he'd tense up with a mixture of hope and apprehension; when they passed by he was never sure whether he was relieved or disappointed.

—Are you ready, are you ready! bawled the bloke in the black vest. He had set up a stepladder by the window and was climbing up it. His mate handed him a hammer and a length of rolled-up cloth.

—Mind and get the bastard straight!

—Are you ready, are you ready!

The one on the ladder tacked an edge of the cloth to the

window frame. Then, with a theatrical sweep of the arm and an ugly cheer, unfurled the makeshift blind – a Union Jack.

Sonia and Parveen, whizzing by happily on their bikes, looked up to see what was causing the commotion, wobbled, crashed into each other and collapsed in a wailing heap at Russell's gate.

SEVEN

Cuisine with Character

—Sometimes I get really pissed off with progress, said
Dawn. Does more harm than good. Look at the primitive tribes they make all those documentaries about,
the ones that live in the jungle or the rain forest or
whatever: they've got along very nicely without
technology and modern medicine. They've got their own
ways of doing things, their own remedies. They know
how to take care of themselves. They always look so
happy, too, laughing and dancing, singing songs. Even
when they're working they're singing songs. Just imagine
anyone in our place singing. And you never hear of any
of those tribal people suffering from depression, do you?
I mean once they've caught enough food for the day,
they just sit around decorating their bodies and telling
stories.

—It might take days to catch enough food for a meal,

Russell replied. And I doubt if it's all love and peace in the jungle.

—No, but still, medicine has a lot to answer for. I mean, take Morris . . .

—No thanks.

—I don't mean *that* way. He's not bad though. If he'd lighten up a bit. And if he really is *untouched* a girl could have some fun.

Morris, at twenty-seven, was reputed to be a virgin. Not from any informed sense of caution, or even religious restraints but — so the gossip went — from lack of opportunity: the boy had been too busy poring over medical textbooks to get around to any hands-on anatomy. As well as a lack of sexual experience, it was also rumoured that the birthday boy had a low tolerance for alcohol and Todd — to verify the rumour — had been plying him with booze.

—By the end of tonight, said Todd, he'll go home with anybody.

—Oh dear!

Dawn giggled tipsily. Dawn worked in reception, which mostly meant answering the phone and making coffee for visitors to the plant. She was employed for her clipped consonants, her eye-catching dress sense — tonight's off-the-shoulder electric blue tube was no exception — and her ability to be charming to any amount of visiting dickheads. Like Morris, being able to hold her drink was clearly not part of Dawn's remit.

—By the way, Fairley, said Todd, I didn't know you were palsy with Ms Manila.

—I'm not.

Todd smirked.

—Really. Hardly know her. Gave me a lift to work the other day. A bloody bumpy ride, I can tell you.

—Mmmnn. Doesn't strike me as a particularly compliant little blossom. But they're a deceptive lot, Fairley. The oriental mind is a mystery.

Todd had spent two weeks in some Thai equivalent of Butlins, a thatched hut complex of some kind; *dirt cheap drink and hordes of tasty and very obliging local chicks* ; and now considered himself an expert on all things oriental, though women and drink were his special areas of interest.

—I tell you, man. Ms Manila I'd avoid like herpes. Take my word for it, give that bitch the body-swerve. Stick with Arlene.

Russell had been prepared to hate the birthday celebrations from the word go. He'd booked the table for Morris weeks ago, before Arlene spilled the beans and moved into the back cellar of Boon's. If he hadn't been off sick, he'd have remembered in time to look for another venue but at such short notice and on the night of a Rugby International, the town stowed out with beer-swilling choirboys in silly hats, it wouldn't have been easy. And what excuse would he have given for changing the venue?

He hadn't been able to taste a thing. Normally this would have been a big disappointment – Russell liked his food – but tonight he couldn't help feeling pleased that Arlene's culinary skills had failed to make any impact on his palate. He'd have been even more pleased if the dinner had been a disaster but since the first mounds of smoked salmon mousse had appeared, nestling on twists of frilly purple lettuce, everybody had been banging on about how good the food was. Why did they have to get all gastronomic tonight? At a works do, drink was the social lubricant. The sight of food usually had some gloomy bugger waxing lyrical about listeria, CJD or E Coli.

He'd never been a great one for socialising at the best of

times. Company, enjoying yourself in it, taking part, entering into the spirit etc usually involved a lot of unnecessary verbal effort and downright idiotic social interaction before anybody was prepared to declare a good night out, and tonight would be no exception. His own company, anywhere but bloody Boon's, would have done him fine. Still, so far, it had gone off remarkably painlessly; so far, he hadn't seen hide nor hair of Arlene. Was she really through the back, sweating and swearing over a hot stove?

Arlene might not have made the food, of course. She might have taken off for the night. Who with? *With whom*: Arlene. Arlene liked to be correct about words. Pity she didn't apply the same standards when it came to human relations. Was lover boy back in town already? According to the listings which Russell scanned obsessively these days, Fox wasn't due to hit town for a week or two. But maybe he'd flown over early to be with his Celtic queen. Maybe while Russell was sitting in Boon's, picking on a grilled fish, Arlene and Frankie boy were simultaneously contributing to a wordless appendix for *Eating Passionfruit in Bed*.

The framed botanical drawings which Arlene had whipped from the bedroom walls when she left him now adorned the corridor leading to the toilets. Otherwise, the place hadn't changed much since he'd last been in. Still the same old upwardly mobile Boon's, with its distempered walls and sanded floors, its scrubbed trestle tables and high-backed chairs upholstered in unbleached calico. He knew the fabric was unbleached calico because Arlene had agonised for weeks about it. One rowdy party was all it took to make her realise the drawback of the pale, absorbent fabric.

Russell's first date with Arlene had been spent at

Boon's. She had invited him down on a Monday night, when the restaurant was closed. It had taken him ages to find the place.

I don't want folk falling in off the street just because it's the first place they see. I want them to make an effort: Arlene.

New to the city – and to the job – he hadn't yet got to grips with the warren-like construction of the Old Town: wynds so narrow you had to walk with your arms pressed to your sides, so steep and on a damp, greasy night, so slippery he'd had to grip the dripping walls to prevent himself skiting down the cobbles. Not only was Boon's at the bottom of a wynd but it was in a cellar. In a city famous for its skyline, how the hell had socialising in dungeons caught on?

That night he'd been hoping for a cosy candlelit dinner but the only food in sight was a plate of cold potatoes Arlene put out for the ghosts she believed haunted the building. She was convinced that Boon's was host to three of them, left over from the seventeenth century, when the Black Death ravaged Europe. At that time an earlier street had run beneath the present High Street and its colonnade of souvenir shops. Archaeologists had opened up part of the old street and discovered, amongst other delights, a section which had been walled off to contain plague victims. On that first date, Arlene had talked incessantly about death by pestilence, which, even for a microbiologist, hadn't been much of a turn-on.

They'd been there for hours and only just got on to ordering brandies and Irish coffees. A hell of a noisy bunch, when they got together. Perhaps it had something to do with having to shout at work to be heard above the machinery. Whatever, it was wearing. Now that the plates had been cleared away he had a space to lay his head on the table – and a powerful desire to do so – or to go, get the hell out. His head was heavy, too heavy but his feet were rehearsing a journey to the door, out under the dripping ivy and swirly nameplate: *BOON'S – Cuisine With Character*, up the slippery cobbles and away.

—Did you get a cake? Russell asked Todd.

—Oh yes. Wait till you see it.

—Cake! said Dawn. I'm stuffed. It's not good for your digestion to eat a lot at night. You should really eat early in the day and then work off the calories. If you eat at night the food just sits in your stomach. It takes ages for the enzymes to break it down. I mustn't think about it. I've got a very vivid imagination, you know. If I start thinking about my insides, I start to see everything pumping and swishing. Is there any more wine?

Unconcerned for evermore about Arlene's unbleached calico chair covers, Russell leaned across the table and sloshed more red into Dawn's glass.

The lights were dimmed – for dramatic effect or because the staff were dropping hints about being keen to get off home. Whatever, it coincided with Todd emerging from the kitchen, holding aloft a cake. The candles flickered atmospherically. Dawn inhaled and exhaled which called most of the men – and it was a predominantly male crowd – to attention. Todd made his way slowly towards the table. The waiters paused briefly in their table-wiping and chair-stacking. Even Lag, the rangy lugubrious dishwasher, in his perennial uniform of distressed tartan, slunk out of the kitchen and took the opportunity to suck on a roll-up. When he caught Russell's eye, he nodded minimally.

Lag the reliable. Silent as the bloody grave. Been with Arlene for years, putting in his hours at the sink, exchanging only the barest dregs of conversation. And behind Lag, Arlene herself was wiping her hands on her already mucky apron. Her pinned-up hair had unravelled into a heavy, lopsided hank. It must have been something about the light, or the time of night, or the booze he'd sunk, or maybe Arlene only appeared fetchingly dishevelled in contrast to Dawn who looked like she'd been gift-wrapped.

Russell's symptoms: irritation, confusion, embarrassment, stubbornness, humiliation, vanity, self-consciousness, self-righteousness . . .

'Happy Birthday to you' was dribbling messily round the table. Morris beamed as the cake was set down in front of him. He was a picture of laddish contentment: cheeks flushed, shirt collar open, his optical headache of a tie dangling like a noose. He drew in his breath, puffed out his twenty-seven-year-old chest and blew violently at the candles, extinguishing the lot. The lights were turned up again and the cheers collapsed into guffaws. The cake – Todd's choice – had been moulded to resemble a life-size pair of tits. Morris, drunk and delighted, held it up so those at the end of the table could get a better look. In a moment of inebriated inspiration, he bit off one of the red sugar nipples. Fired up by the roar of approval, disgust and hilarity rumbling round the table, Morris didn't stop at the symbolic gesture; swallowing the fondant tit, he began to devour the flesh-coloured globe. Under the icing there was some kind of creamy stuff which got all over his nose but he gobbled on, oblivious to party protocol.

—You've got to share it, Morris, said Dawn.

—It's mine!

—It's bad luck not to share your cake. I know somebody who didn't share his birthday cake and something really terrible happened to him.

—Save yourself for the real thing, said Todd.

The real thing – also Todd's choice – was through the back, getting into her gear.

—Is there a knife? said Todd. We need a knife.

The cutlery had all been cleared away. Lag, Arlene, and the waiters had drifted back to the kitchen.

—What happened? Morris mumbled through cream and crumbs.

—Oh, it was really terrible, said Dawn. Terrible. You wouldn't want it to happen to your worst enemy.

—Has anybody got a knife? There'll be nothing left to cut soon.

—You shouldn't tamper with luck, Morris. You never know what unseen forces are working all around you.

Russell, who was all too aware of unknown forces working around him, reluctantly made his way to the kitchen. Arlene was standing by the oven wielding two long-bladed knives.

—Take your pick, she said.

—Either will do.

—Do me a favour, said Arlene. Choose, will you?

—Okay, okay.

Russell chose the bigger knife. It was a big cake, at least, it had been.

—I didn't really expect to see you here.

—If my cover hadn't called in sick, I wouldn't be here. How was the food?

—Fine.

—Fine.

—Very nice. Fine.

—You don't sound very definite.

—I'm not a very definite sort of bloke.

—Tell me about it. I just appreciate a bit of verbal feedback.

—Don't we all. A simple *Hello*. A *How have you been since I dumped you?* But no, food food food.

—Hello, Russell. How have you been? It's not really the time to talk, is it? I ask about the food because I need to know what people think. If nobody ever says anything, all I have to go on is what's left on the plates.

—No complaints. Nothing to worry about. Everything was fine.

—I don't want it to be *fine*. I don't want it to be *not bad*.

—So you're a perfectionist. That's your problem. I couldn't taste much but that's just me. Is the lassie about ready? The birthday boy's plastered.

—He'd better not puke in my dining room. I'll give *the lassie* a shout.

—She wasn't my idea, said Russell.

—Hm. I'm not having this kind of thing again. It's tacky and pathetic.

—I'd say screwing a stranger and telling him all about your current boyfriend's personal habits might also fall under that definition.

—Not now, Russell. Please. I'm working, remember?

—So when exactly will you talk? When might you fit me into your hectic schedule?

Russell's symptoms: annoyance (acute), hope (vain), discomfort (severe), pride (hurt)

As he returned to the table with one of Arlene's Kitchen Devils, Russell's silhouette ballooned across the archway like that of a cartoon villain.

After the ritual slicing up of what remained of the cake, the lights were dimmed again and the real thing made her entrance – as a policewoman in stiletto heels; conversation became constipated. Sergeant Vi Venom – her name was stitched across her chest – turned up the volume on her sound system, marched up to the table, grabbed the birthday boy by the tie, pecked his cream-smeared cheeks and began to gyrate her arse like a piece of well-oiled machinery.

> Boom badda BOOM boom badda BOOM
> Badda badda BOOM badda boom BOOM
> *Do ya think I'm sexy, do ya think I'm cute*
> *Do ya wanna fuck me in my birthday suit.*

Something like that. The days of innuendo, of subtlety had long died out of song lyrics. And – by the looks of it – strip routines. Russell slugged at his brandy. There wasn't much point in trying not to watch. He was close enough to see Vi Venom's goose pimples.

She was a big girl, blonde and busty, with a sun-bed tan, an intimidating leer and – it was soon revealed – a befuddling arrangement of buckles and thongs under her uniform. The birthday boy was invited to do some unbuckling. He didn't say yes and he didn't say no but his hands flew forward and grabbed on to the first thing they came in contact with – the leather tassels suspended from Vi Venom's twin peaks.

For a reputed virgin, the boy seemed forward enough. But other than hanging on to the tassels and tugging clumsily – which Vi tolerated for a while with professional disinterest – Morris seemed at a loss, fumbling and slobbering and hanging on until she extricated herself, unhitched her halter top and slung it round Morris' neck. The birthday boy gasped and sniggered and had to be restrained from taking a bite out of the real thing. Vi unzipped her skirt and there, alongside the suspenders and tattoos of bluebirds, bleeding hearts and a coiling snake were the obligatory whip and cuffs, clipped to a thick chain.

——Missing the climax? said Arlene.

 ——Yeah, well, what's new.

 ——Not your type?

 ——Wouldn't chuck her out of bed. Not that I'd be likely to get her in it, either, without breaking the bank.

 ——A man who knows his limitations.

EIGHT

Heart of Midlothian

He wasn't overweight. He could lose a few pounds maybe but so could most of Arlene's customers. For somebody who made her living from filling bellies, her attitude to the expanding waistband was self-defeating to say the least. As for the lardball Fox had turned him into, that was just a piece of bloody nonsense:

> 'Little's body had a yellowish, greasy sheen, like fat which had solidified in a pan. When he walked, he wobbled. Seeing him naked, Iona felt compelled to turn off the light immediately.'

Christ, it wouldn't have hurt to have been a mite more generous to the bloke you shafted. But no, not a single attractive feature was attributed to Leslie Little.

On the pavement outside the Sheriff Courts, in clothes

too thin for the bitter wind which skirled down the hill from the Castle battlements, a restless crowd of defendants waited for their names to be called. They huddled over cigarettes, cupping the glowing tips between chapped fingers, blocking the pavement. A flame-cheeked baby, cocooned in a puffy pink snowsuit, sucked furiously on a dummy as its buggy was shoogled – none too gently – between its mother and father, neither of whom looked old enough for legitimate sex.

—Ah'm tellin you, Lenny, stay away frae ma bairn.

—She's mine tae. Ma wee lassie. Ma wee darlin, eh? Ah helped bring her intae the world.

—Your bit didnae take much effort.

—It did too.

The father bent down to the baby and googled at it.

—Gie's a wee smile, Natasha. Come oan. Take oot that fuckin plug.

He yanked the dummy out of the baby's mouth. The baby was silent for the time it took to draw in enough breath to scream. It drew in enough breath to scream very loudly. The mother chucked her glowing fag end in the gutter. A brace of advocates, engaged in animated, engrossing conversation, breezed through the open door and cut a swathe through the disgruntled crowd.

—Gie her that fuckin dummy. She's needin a sleep. Shut up, Natasha.

—They things gie the bairns buck teeth, so they dae. Ah dinnae want ma wee lassie lookin like Bugs Bunny.

—She hasnae got ony teeth yet, Lenny.

—Got lungs aw the same. Great wee pair o lungs, Natasha. You'll be yellin for the Hibees in a coupla years.

—Ma bairn's no goin near a fucking pitch. Ma bairn's gonnae be brought up proper, right.

—Ma bairn, ma bairn. D'ye no ken the facts o life? Ah keep tellin ye, it takes two tae make a bairn.

—So how come it only takes one tae look efter it?

—Fuck off.

Russell stepped off the pavement and dodged through the traffic which rumbled down the High Street in a solid column. He could still hear baby Natasha bawling long after he'd turned the corner. Just as well he and Arlene had never got round to reproducing. As he passed the Heart of Midlothian, he added his spit to the puddle of lucky phlegm.

NINE

Bloodstone, No, Not Bloodstone

By the time she arrived, Russell realised that the place Arlene had chosen to meet him was a hopeless venue for any kind of private conversation. Set in the crypt of the cathedral, it was a low-ceilinged café with rackety flagstone floors and lighting more suitable for an interrogation. There was a persistent, angry clatter of crockery from the kitchen. A stone's throw from the courts, the place was packed with dark-suited legal people and uniformed police, shuffling papers, cracking jokes and filling the room with self-importance. The two of them couldn't even get a table to themselves.

—Couldn't we go somewhere else? Somewhere quieter?

—Nowhere central's quiet at this time. Anyway, I don't have time to trail around looking for somewhere which might suit you better.

—Well, thanks, thanks a lot.

It wasn't an encouraging beginning. Arlene set down her teapot, cup and saucer and returned the tray to the stack. It seemed to take her an age to actually sit down and even when she did, she busied herself with her tea things in an irritatingly deliberate, methodical way and avoided eye contact.

She was wearing a new shade of lipstick – a ghoulish reddish black or blackish red, like bloodstone – no, not bloodstone, haematite – and her hair, freshly chopped across the forehead and along the jaw line, had a purplish tint. All trace of grey had been eliminated. She wore nothing but black. Even her earrings were ugly black barbs; he'd seen similar items in a scruffy martial arts' shop near the flat which had recently lost its licence for selling illegal weaponry.

Arlene looked good in an unsettling, irritating way. Too bloody good.

—So, she said. How've you been?

—Hellish. Went down with some god-awful bug. Raging temperature, delirium, pains everywhere, nightmares, hallucinations, you name it. Made me feel like jumping off a bridge if only I had the energy to get to one. Couldn't get to the phone at one point. You didn't, by any unlikely chance, phone last week?

—Not me.

—Oh. So you didn't try to get in touch.

—I had problems of my own to attend to. Sorry.

—Please don't be sorry. What is there to be sorry about? Absolutely no reason at all to be sorry. I'm the one who should be sorry, the one who is sorry, let me tell you. And you had problems of your own. Of course. How insensitive of me. Life elsewhere goes on willy-nilly. Life *is* elsewhere.

Arlene sighed loudly, looked around at everyone but him.

—It's true what they say. A good suit does wonders for a man.

—Life is elsewhere, he repeated. I like that. Short, to the point.

—It isn't original.

—What is, except sin.

Arlene sighed again. She was good at sighing.

—Never miss a chance do you?

—Beggars can't be choosers.

—As your granny used to say.

—Leave my granny out of this. She's been dead for years. So you didn't phone?

—No, Russell, I didn't.

— . . .

— . . .

—These problems you had. Medical were they? Of the sexually transmitted variety?

—We can do this by letter, said Arlene.

—Yes, said Russell. Solicitor's letter. I've already found someone who's very interested in my situation.

—Really.

—Really. But please, do tell me your problems.

—They don't concern you.

—No? The thing is, I couldn't help noticing as I was reading *Eating Passionfruit in Bed*, that no protective measures were mentioned on pages 24–34, or pages 57–71. Considering the deluge of nauseatingly intimate details included, I can only conclude that government-recommended prophylactics were not used.

—Poetic licence, it's called. Descriptions of condoms being put on didn't suit the tone of the passages . . .

—The tone of unbridled lust . . .

Arlene lit a cigarette and began puffing clouds of smoke directly into his face.

—Or on pages 186–199.

—What an attentive reader you are.

—Oh yes, Arlene, very attentive. Nothing has escaped me, nothing. Even what the critics say has been taken note of.

—I never read the papers. Too busy keeping the business going.

Russell dug into his pocket and extracted some crushed cuttings.

—Let me bring you up to date, then. *SOGGY SHEETS*.

—Fucksake, Russell.

—Indeed. *SOGGY SHEETS*.

Russell handed over the extract, folded his arms and glared at random customers of the café while Arlene raced through the following:

Adultery is such an everyday affair in fiction – as in the real lives of the rich and famous, not to mention the poor and unheard of – that any writer foolish enough to make it not just the linch-pin of his narrative but in this case the entire narrative, has his work cut out for him to say the least. But Franklin B. Fox doesn't fret about that. Nor does he restrain himself from making his main character a novelist who, one shudders to think, bears more than a passing resemblance to the author himself.

The book is ostensibly set in Edinburgh, Scotland's Festival City, which Guy Rightman – aka Franklin Fox – visits to launch a book. In his all-too-brief foray into the city, he experiences the Scottish weather – a bitter, hop-flavoured wind and driving rain – does his promotional bit in a bookshop, picks up a stranger – a local woman – and lures her to his room in a fusty hotel where he rediscovers himself through extensive carnal knowledge of the said stranger. The 'passionfruit' of the title is a motif which is squeezed to a juiceless rind. Needless to say, in this dreich northern city – the rain doesn't let up for the entire novel – such succulent morsels aren't in plentiful supply, though Fox's imagination is positively dripping, his creative juices coaxed into spurting forth by his willing and tireless Muse:

Her hair was the blue-black of a crow's wing, her skin blue-white and as delicately freckled as a wild bird's egg. Her back had the contours of an ivory violin . . .

Yes, lads, we all know an Iona Rivers, don't we?
And when Iona stands at the window of the hotel bedroom – in between sessions on the by now unimaginably soggy sheets – to gaze at the rain plashing down – Fox takes his lusty hero on a trip down sensuality lane. A case of writing with one hand perhaps. Be advised, Mr Fox, two hands are better than one, for most things.

—That's just one stupid person's opinion. Anyway, it's not me, is it? I mean it's nothing like your description of me. You see some thick-skinned bitch . . .

—And he sees bird's eggs and ivory violins.

—It's made up, Russell. It's got hardly anything to do with the real me.

—Or the real me.

—It's got fuck all to do with the real you.

—So you admit it? You admit that it's a travesty of the truth?

—It's just a story!

—Aye. A story. Have a look at what Fergus Burnturk thinks.

Russell slapped a second flaccid scrap of newsprint on top of the first and began to drink his coffee noisily. Arlene lit a cigarette, inhaled deeply and reluctantly made a start on:

CALEDONIAN LOVE FEAST

Eating Passionfruit in Bed: a fairly exotic title for a tale set in stodgy Auld Reekie, isn't it? How many of us are passionfruit eaters in or out of bed – I for one am not even sure I'd recognise this far-flung delicacy – but, really, shouldn't we be talking white pudding suppers or, if we want to be fancy, smoked salmon and crowdie? Well now, some of what happens in this book might also strike local readers as unlikely too but the world's a big place, people get up to all kinds of daft things and what goes on between two people in private, well, everybody knows there's different strokes for different folks. But do we really need to know what all these wee foibles actually boil down to – or in this case bubble up to? And the kind of foibles Mr Fox dwells on for the lion's share of 333 pages might come as a bit of a shock for some intrepid members of the public! Definitely an entertainment for randy readers but not a lot here for those of us who prefer a rattling good yarn. A good stocking filler for some but for Auntie Mary, stick to Turkish Delight.

—A stocking-filler?

—Of the fishnet rather than woolly variety, I'd say.

—Well, said Arlene, I wouldn't trust anyone who didn't know what a passionfruit looked like, in this day and age. What's happened to their curiosity? You walk past a fruit shop, you see these wrinkled little miseries and you think, what are they? You maybe see them a couple of times before you get around to asking about them, but you do, don't you? Something edible that you've never seen before, looks like shit and turns out to be called passionfruit, well, I mean, where's his argument? People like that make me want to run a burger bar.

—That's crap, Arlene.

—How d'you mean?

—I mean, it's crap. You'd hate to run a burger bar. Far too functional for you. You are talking crap.

—That's three times you've said crap. You're fixated on crap.

—Well, that makes two of us.

—Since when did you start reading book reviews?

—Here's the last one.

—It better be the fucking last one.

Arlene stubbed out her cigarette and lit another.

—Smoking a lot these days, said Russell.

—Shut up, said Arlene.

SPITTING OUT THE PIPS OF PASSION

Iona has a dull, dependable boyfriend, Leslie, who works at a lab. The boyfriend is bald, running to fat and insecure. Iona's mercurial personality has been too long constrained by the flagging relationship with Leslie and finds the seductively different Guy Rightman irresistible. A night of passion ensues and the hitherto jaded Rightman rediscovers his libido. What Iona feels about the whole affair is veiled in a mist of Celtic susurrus. We find out a great deal more about her body than her mind, partly because she doesn't say much and because we stay with her literary lover's angle on things the whole way through. Does Iona get a fair deal? Do her mostly passive roles in the sex scenes – more or less the only scenes – suggest that women are being yet again portrayed as victims even in a position of relative strength? Is she turning the tables on morality and making a stand for women to make the most of their sexuality? Read it, readers, and decide for yourselves.

Arlene sipped her tea, sighed and stared into her cup.

—Well, Arlene, what's your opinion?

—The book is meant to be funny.

—Funny, oh yes. Hilarious. I crack up with helpless mirth every time I think of my personal life squirted across the pages of that piece of crap.

—There you go again.

—I expect it'll sell like hot cakes. People relish the misfortunes of others, the humiliations. They are reassured to know that they themselves didn't sink to such depths of deception.

—Isn't it depths of depravity? Isn't that the phrase you're looking for?

—Deception has its depths. And its shallows.

—You're wasted at the lab, Russell. Why don't you consider advertising, or the ministry, before it's too late? I mean, I know we're on church property, Russell, but really . . .

—Sorry. I'm sure you have so many other, more pressing things to do than listen to me banging on.

—Well, to be honest . . .

—Oh, please be honest. Change the habit of a lifetime.

Arlene sighed again, let her teaspoon clatter into her half-empty cup, buttoned up her black jacket, slipped her fingers into her black velvet gloves, snapped her handbag shut and left, the heavy oak door thudding shut behind her. The cops at the other end of the table lowered their heads, stirred their coffee and smirked.

Russell spread his elbows on the table and glared at a tiny stained glass window, set deep in the wall. The walls of the cathedral must, he realised, be about a foot thick. He wasn't going to rush off anywhere. He was just going to sit where he was, as if he'd meant Arlene to walk out on him, as if he were the one who'd scored a point. That was what their relationship amounted to now. He was just going to sit where he was. He was in no hurry. He had all day. The rest of his life.

The cops got up, smirked again in his direction, and left. As if on cue, the legal people also rose, slipping files under the arms of cashmere coats. Their showy exodus was followed by a brief, still moment before the staff emerged from the kitchen and began clearing tables. The place took on a more mundane air. Crockery still sounded as if it were being dropped from a great height into a dry sink in the kitchen but it had a more gentle, lackadaisical rhythm and, in the dining area, conversation was now muted to a murmur.

An elderly couple in identical tweed jackets sat and stared past each other until the woman reached out to brush a crumb from the man's sleeve.

—Lay off Edith.

—You should take more pride in your appearance, Eddie.

—Who's looking?

—I am, Eddie.

—No, you're not. You're looking at the poster on the wall.

—What poster?

—About the Bring and Buy Sale. You've missed it. It was last week.

—Better than watching you make a mess of yourself. It's embarrassing being with a man who can't get his food into his mouth.

—It's embarrassing being with a woman who can't keep from dabbing her hanky all over you.

—It was just one tiny dab. You do exaggerate, Eddie.

—It may be, Edith, that if you dabbed with a bit more imagination, I wouldn't have to exaggerate.

TEN

A Hideous Jig

He is in Boon's; he knows it is Boon's but candles drip on raw wood trestles and blackened greasy walls drip with condensation. In the middle of the room, a fire spits; at its hearth, a pair of lean dogs snap and grizzle over a large bone. The dirt floor is littered with peelings, fruit pips, fish heads, scraps of gristle, dog shit. Flies fizz and blister a steaming turd. A colony of rats noses through the pickings, nonchalant, proprietorial. Boon's, but no art nouveau, no nouvelle cuisine for the nouveau riche; a beggar's banquet. At the table the toothless, shoeless and possibly mindless eat, drink and are more than merry; hysterical in fact, swilling down blue black wine and ramming food down their gullets, as if each mouthful were their last. On a nearby bench a plump young woman and a vigorous young man gorge on each other. Seeing them so engrossed, a fat man in a gaping shirt, cheeks red as tomatoes, tongue wetly circling his mouth, plucks a turkey leg from the table and shoves it down the young woman's cleavage.

The woman squints at her breasts, pale and quivering like twin scoops of junket. The turkey leg glistens with grease. Her chin sinks into the folds of her neck. Her mouth droops open, tongue curls greedily towards the rounded tips of grey-pink bone. She pushes aside her young man and spreads her legs. The diners leer and drool. A second turkey leg is shoved roughly into the depths of her filthy petticoats. Panting – from lust or lack of breath – the tomato-cheeked man, his free hand closing on his crotch, pumps the plump woman full of turkey meat. Her moans are a mixture of pleasure and pain.

In an unlit booth, a wasted woman begins to beat a sombre, ponderous rhythm on an empty beer keg. The dogs raise their narrow heads. The rats are oblivious. The diners sup from mugs of ale or slump into their plates. A voice, a cold, steely voice cuts through the belches and guffaws, the moans of misery and desire. The diners stagger to their feet and form a ramshackle chain. As one touches another, their rags crumble to the ground like long dead skin, revealing flesh riddled with dark blotches and swellings. A dry, rasping laughter crackles round the cavernous room as the procession lurches into a slow, hideous jig. Tongues balloon from mouths, lewd and stupid. The revelry swells but still doesn't drown out the ponderous dead beat of the drum nor the icy plainsong of the Pest Maiden, a tall, gaunt, hollow-eyed bag of bones, her distended shadow slithering across the floor: Here I have always been, waiting in the dark. My time has come again.

The fire hisses, gasps. The room is hot as a furnace. The procession stops at the bench. The leader stretches out his cankered hands. The fat man falls to his knees, the displaced lover covers his eyes and the plump woman throws back her head and screams . . .

Arlene is standing at the door of the kitchen. Her apron is bloody as a butcher's. With a sweep of her arm, she clears the table.

—So what have you decided on then? Listeria, salmonella, E Coli, CJD? Or would you prefer something more traditional?

E L E V E N

Antarctica

—Hate to do this to you, but your first stop's Antarctica, said Todd. The night man's fucked up. If these figures are right, the power's been off in the deep freeze for at least two hours, can you believe it? Of course you can, anything's possible around here, isn't it? Chasing your arse round this labyrinth and losing track of it, that's not just possible, it's par for the course.

—I should have stayed in bed.

—Me too, said Todd. If you catch sight of Bobby Doyle – he hasn't clocked out yet – tell him he's dead meat.

To get to the deep freeze he had to go out of the main building and cross the loading bay. The sky was leaden, the air damp, close to freezing point. Delivery men, made idle by the cock-up, were sitting about in their vans, grabbing a fag and a skim at the paper. They were used to delays. All kinds of things could hold up production but a problem with Antarctica was no small matter. The last thing Russell wanted to do was worry about work; he'd enough trouble tolerating the job at the best of times. Toleration? *Toleration leads to apathy*: Arlene. But what else could he do but put up with the limits that he lived between? What else was there to do? Nowhere much else to go, and no chance of promotion where he was, he knew that, everybody knew their place at the centre. There was a clearly defined strat-ification, inflexible as a caste system. You weren't literally born to it but you might as well have been. A plant opera-tor shovelling slush puppy into the chute hour after hour hadn't a hope in hell of ending up in management. Slush puppy was Todd's name for the semi-frozen plasma which did, in fact, look very like pissed-upon snow.

Forty degrees below and by Christ did you know it when you stepped inside. The heavy steel door clicked behind him. Flecks of frost clung to the rows of stacked packing cases and whirled down from the ceiling in a blizzard. The cold cut through his clothes like a scalpel and in seconds he was chittering. This was not the place to loiter; do what needs doing and get the hell out. Imagine choosing to spend months on end in this kind of tempera-ture, even in a down-padded suit and fur-lined boots, even if you were extending the boundaries of human knowledge.

If he hadn't skidded on a patch of ice, he might have missed the night watchman who was slumped between a couple of packing cases, blue mouth hanging open, blue hands clenched together as if in prayer. Christ, was he dead? He wasn't moving and looked a lot more dead than alive, the limbs stiff and skewed, as if rigor mortis had already set in. Ice crystals glinted around his mouth and nose and rose up from the stubble on his chin like frosty peaks.

—Bobby! Bobby! Let's get out of here man!

Nothing. No sign of breathing. He was barely breathing himself he was so shit-scared. He wanted to get help, to be not the only one dealing with this but there was no time; even if the man wasn't dead yet he would be very soon if he stayed in the icebox. Russell had no time to do anything but fill his lungs with killer cold air, grab the rigid, icy arms and hoist and drag, hoist and drag. Bobby was a wee stick of a guy but Christ he was heavy, heavy enough to be dead.

Russell had forgotten anything he'd ever known about first aid. Why wasn't everyone taught these things at school, taught them properly, just in case? All those months spent on cosines and quadratic equations and just one afternoon visit from the Red Cross and a demonstration of how to administer the kiss of life to a rubber dummy. He must be right; he must move Bobby. The cold would kill him if it hadn't already done so.

Every second could be Bobby's last and their progress was so slow, so bloody hellish slow; his own arms felt numb and rigid as he inched the night man's body across the frosty floor, ice crystals adhering to Bobby's stiff overalls, a blue-white rime on his bristles.

When the heavy electronic door didn't open immediately, Russell's heart began to hammer painfully against his ribs, the red and green lights of the sensor blurred into white. A fault in the door, there could be a fault and how long would it take for anyone to notice? He lowered Bobby to the floor and began to bang on the re-inforced steel. When the door hummed and slid back, the dreich November weather was as welcome as a summer's day.

—Breathe, you bastard, breathe.

Russell glared at Bobby, willing him to show some sign of life, but Bobby's frozen, unblinking eyes just glared back.

—Are you sure that's what you're supposed to do?

—Haven't a bloody clue, man, but I'm not standing here watching a boy die before my eyes.

—Ah read somewhere that wi certain injuries, you're no supposed tae move the victim.

Russell had raised the alarm, sent for the doctor and enlisted Jake and Davey – delivery boys – to help roll Bobby on to a wooden pallet and carry him into the corridor of the main building. He'd taken off his jacket and wrapped it round Bobby's chest and was rubbing his arms and legs, trying to rub some heat into the man's body.

—What if he's deid already? said Jake.

—I couldn't very well leave him in the deep freeze, could I?

—Naw, but now he's oot, he maybe better sort of thaw by himsel, ken, said Davey.

—Aye, said Jake. See hypothermia, it's dead tricky. Mind that tragedy in the Bosphorus? That ferry that went doon a couple o winters back. Did ye no read aboot it? They got all the folk oot the water – and it must have been fucking icy man, the Bosphorus is no the Caribbean – three days it took tae find them but they were all alive when they were picked up. Amazing they survived that long. They were pulled oot the water, wrapped up in blankets and given hot drinks straight away and look what happened.

—What happened? said Davey.

—Snuffed it, didn't they? said Jake. Every last one of them. Something tae dae wi the warming process. It was too quick like, too much o a sudden change. Like you dinnae thaw oot a frozen chicken by sticking it in the oven.

—But a frozen chicken's deid already, said Davey. You're no tryin tae bring it back tae life.

—Aye but the principle's the same, isn't it? And maybe this boy's deid an all.

—Dinnae say that, said Davey. Ah widnae want tae think ah wis handling a deid body. Maybe ah just have, right enough, that's a thought.

—Could you just keep your fucking thoughts to yourself, said Russell.

—Nae call tae be cheeky, pal, said Davey. We're just rallying roon till the doctor gets here, ken.

—Aye, said Jake. Then we're offski. This is naethin tae dae wi us, ken. Ah'm no sure we're covered for shifting bodies, deid or alive.

—That doctor's fair taking his time, is he no?

Russell continued rubbing Bobby's chest and belly frantically, gasping and sweating and cursing from the exertion. By the time Everett arrived with Morris, quite a crowd had assembled.

—Clear a space, said Everett. Move aside, everybody. Give Dr Morrison a chance to do his job.

Everett began flapping his long arms at the spectators, shooing them away like sheep or birds. Morris didn't look as if he wanted a chance to do his job; he eyed the inert nightwatchman warily, as if he might leap up and ask him to name every bone in the body.

—The ambulance should be here any minute, Everett added, as he peered anxiously down the driveway.

—That's if there areny any traffic jams doon the toon, said Jake.

—Aye, said Davey. Ken when ah was on my way over the morn, the road was chock-a-block fae start tae finish.

Ah blame the cooncil. Diggin up the bloody High Street for months.

—And for what, ah'd like tae ken. No tae widen the bloody road, aw no. Nothin sensible like that. Naw, they're narrowing the bastard, narrowing it. Tae slow doon the fuckin traffic.

The icicles had melted from Bobby's chin but otherwise there were no noticeable changes to the body by the time the ambulance swung into the drive. Morris checked Bobby's pulse, respiration, shone a torch into his eyes and tapped his knees with a hammer; there were no apparent signs of life. Everett ordered everybody back to work but nobody did any more than step back a pace or two. The ambulancemen behaved as if they had TV cameras trained on them, moving in as a coordinated team, ignoring Everett's attempts to speak to them. They swaddled Bobby in several fleecy blankets, bundled him on to a stretcher, slid him into the ambulance, motioned to Morris to climb in the back and pulled the door shut.

After a swift reverse turn, the ambulance wailed down the drive, past the blue lady in her test tube, the bulldozers, the security cameras. As the siren faded, Russell was sure that he could hear Imelda howling.

—Wasting their breath, said Davey. It's the mortuary they should be heading tae.

—No, but see with hypothermia, ye cannae tell by appearances, said Jake. Cannae make any diagnosis before they warm the body. Like ah said, same principle as a frozen chicken.

T W E L V E

Sick-Heart Hero

Russell was shivering so violently that he could barely get the coffee into his mouth.

—Hey, Rusty, hey!

Muriel waved a lit cigarette in the air and grinned.

—Can I join you?

She laid her cup on the table and pulled out a chair for herself.

—So how does it feel to save a life? Did Big Boots give you a medal or just a crummy patriarchal pat on the back?

So much for peace and quiet. Muriel's voice was like a tinful of razor blades.

—I might have saved a corpse, Muriel. Morris couldn't get a pulse or anything.

—Bobby's alive. Came round in the ambulance. Everett just phoned through to the lab, issuing emergency tests on everything. Talk about bolting the gate when the horse has jumped the fence.

—Shutting the gate when the horse has bolted.

—Yeah, yeah. Okay. It's my second language, right?

—Are you sure?

—Sure I'm sure. Morris called from the hospital. You're a hero, boy.

—I don't feel like a hero.

—Don't you feel proud? It's a big thing to save a life. I know that.

—I feel like shit.

—That man will always be in your debt.

—I doubt if he'll see it that way.

Muriel stubbed out her cigarette and leaned forward.

—You know what I think?

—No, Muriel, I don't.

—I think you're depressed.

—I don't get depressed.

—Bullshit. You want a ride home tonight? said Muriel.

—The bus is fine.

—It's slow and boring. Meet me at the car park. Unless your girlfriend will be jealous. Arlene, isn't it? I used to see her at the gym but I quit. Couldn't take the strip lights and the noise. Too much like this place.

—Oh Arlene won't be jealous. Arlene couldn't care less. She . . . we, we've split up.

—Aaaahhh. No wonder you look so sick. You got plans for tonight?

—Not that I know of.

—Okay so tonight you come to my place. I'll cook spicy food.

—I don't like spicy food, Muriel.

—Never mind what you like. Spicy food is good for

heroes with sick hearts. I know. I eat it all the time. See how well I am?

Muriel grinned again.

Why in God's name had he told her about Arlene? Until now he'd managed to avoid the subject and had intended to continue avoiding it as long as possible. He'd been doing pretty well in that respect. Even after Morris' bash at Boon's, nobody had been any the wiser about the break-up.

—So you'll come? said Muriel.

—I'll be rubbish company by tonight.

—Who said company? I said food, that's all. In my country it's an insult to refuse food. You can lose your head! But if you have something better to do . . .

—It's not that.

He hardly knew the woman and wasn't at all sure that he wanted to get to know her any better. He shouldn't accept her offer. It was asking for trouble. A woman whose man had skedaddled, a work colleague. A recipe for disaster. Then again, a home-cooked meal was very tempting . . .

—Think I'm gonna make a pass at you over the curry? Think I'm some poor lonely lady trying to trap a man by filling his belly? A tired trick, that one. Look, you think about it.

Russell squirmed in his seat as Todd and Everett came down the corridor, deep in conversation. Everett's free hands flew out from his sides like wings and both men wore the tight-lipped smiles which Russell knew meant trouble. As Todd passed the table, he smirked at Muriel.

—Asshole, she said. That bloody Todd Stalker is a number one asshole.

—He's got his good points.

Muriel stabbed her cigarette at the air between them. Little flakes of ash drifted towards Russell's coffee.

—You're a man. Me, I'm a woman. A Filipina.

—I know that Muriel, said Russell.

—*I know that Muriel.* So what do you know? Do you know that in some dictionaries, a definition of Filipina is 'household servant'?

—Really?

—Yeah really. And that's the definition your got-his-good-points VO likes to use. On top of that, he thinks that when a woman says no, she means yes. So just what do you goddamn know? You know shit, Mr Hero, that's what.

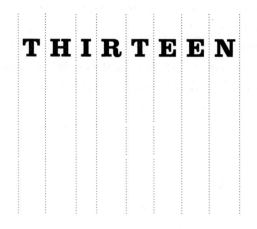

THIRTEEN

Blood Pressure

—It's me.

—What d'you want, Arlene?

—Just a quick word.

—Of course. A quick word from Arlene. Is it important? This number's for emergencies only, Arlene, and we've got one right here. At least we had this morning.

—I've only got a minute, Russell.

—Five years together and you can only spare a minute. The law of diminishing returns.

—Do you have to be so difficult?

—Did you hear what I said? We had an emergency here. A real one. Life and death, Arlene. Don't you want to know what happened?

—Of course I'd love to know but I really am pushed for time. We're fully booked for lunch, short-staffed in the kitchen *and* the dining room. On top of that, the salmon hasn't arrived and because we don't have it, everybody will order it.

—Dear, dear, what a tragedy.

—Sarcasm doesn't suit you, Russell. It just sounds, well pathetic.

—I suppose that's because I'm a pathetic person. *More to be pitied than reviled.* Isn't that how your wizard-with-words lover-boy put it? Still, I might have saved somebody's life today.

—Really. You'll have to tell me about it sometime but not now, Russell, I'm sorry but not now. I've too much to do. My work may seem trivial to you, but the buck stops here, the buck stops at me, Russell.

—At least it knows where to stop.

—Listen, Russell, I'm calling about the flat. I want it sold. Asap. My plans have changed.

—Your plans. What about me? What about my plans? Christ, I've enough on my plate without house-hunting.

—It's got to be done. The sooner it's sorted out, the sooner you'll be free of me.

—It wasn't me who was in such a hurry to be free in the first place, was it?

—Sorry, Russell, okay, sorry. Things have changed.

—It wasn't me who changed.

—No. You didn't. That was part of the problem.

—What d'you mean?

—Never mind, Russell, forget it.

—Doesn't contributing to the mortgage – *your* mortgage – for five years give me a bit more say in all this?

—You'll get your share. Don't worry, Russell, I won't cheat you.

—You already have cheated me.

—By the way, I'm sending Lag round to do some

decorating. The place needs to be done up before I put it on the market.

—Oh no. That kid is not messing up the place I live in.

—The place you live in is hardly an ideal home. The last time I saw it, it was a total tip.

—As I told you, Arlene, I've been ill. I've barely been able to feed myself, far less get enthusiastic about house-keeping. It's not easy being alone when you're ill, Arlene. I don't think you quite understand that. I mean, you've never really done it, have you, never had to get by on your own.

—I'm doing it now, Russell. In far from comfortable conditions.

—Never had to sweat a night out, thinking you weren't going to see the morning. You may not know this, but millions of people have died of flu. Millions. The virus is a genius, Arlene.

—Christ, Russell, I don't have time for a biochemistry lesson. I've got lunches to make. Lots and lots of lunches.

—Caterers can't afford to ignore biochemistry . . . how do you know the flat's a tip?

—I came round to pick up a couple of things. Nothing that could possibly belong to you.

—I've got rights, you know. And I don't have anywhere else to go.

—I'm not doing you any favours by letting you hang on there indefinitely.

—So you're doing me a favour by pushing me into the street.

—In the long run, you'll thank me for it.

—Fuck off.

—Start over somewhere else, Russell. It's the only way. I've got to go. There's a problem in the kitchen.

—Christ, all this drama about a bit of fancy food. You've lost all sense of perspective.

—I've got to go, Russell,

—If some overstuffed suit doesn't get his salmon in Mussolini sauce, you act like the sky's going to fall in . . .

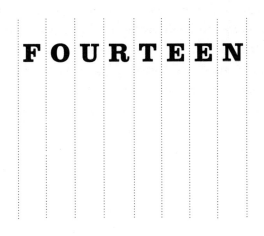

FOURTEEN

Burntisland

Imelda flung herself out of the passenger door as soon as Russell opened it and scrabbled up the track, barking madly.

—Bloody rabbits, said Muriel. Ate all my carrots this year, ruined my peas. One day I'm gonna start shooting.

—You need a gun for that.

—Got one. Welcome to my home.

Muriel handed Russell a sooty bucket, gesturing vaguely towards the darkness.

—Get me some coal, will you?

When she said she lived in the middle of nowhere, she hadn't been exaggerating. They'd left the winding country road ages ago and must have bumped up several miles of a potholed farm track. Away from the weak arc of lamplight above the cottage door was nothing but cold, overwhelming country darkness. A cobwebby drizzle clung to

Russell's hands and face. Reluctantly, he stretched out a hand to feel for the coal shed but instead made contact with the dog's damp, snuffling nose. Muriel was still unloading her messages from the van.

Even he had to bend his head to get through the front door of the cottage. These places had certainly been built for small, houseproud people. The windowsills were at knee height and there was just enough room in the living room for the basics in furniture. Muriel was small enough but houseproud she was not. Imelda had been casting her coat over the carpet and the couch for so long that both were matted and grey. The corners of the window frames were encrusted with an entire summer's worth of spider webs and desiccated flies. On the ledge stood a bunch of long-dead flowers. He put down the bucket of coal and began to lay the fire.

Muriel's living room was more like a man's place than a woman's. A shotgun hung on its strap above the fire-place alongside a torch and a pair of binoculars. On the mantelpiece, cartridges were lined up like poker chips. Otherwise, on sagging, makeshift shelves, there were books, stacks of them, in English, French and a language he didn't recognise, which had been gathering dust and soot from the fire for some time. He was relieved to see that most had the drab, functional appearance of textbooks. Still, as Muriel chopped and stirred in the kitchen, he checked through her entire library. No *Eating Passionfruit in Bed* but *The Free Lunch* was there, next to a dog-eared John Fowles.

The rice simmered in the pan, the smell of fresh ginger pricked Russell's nostrils and Imelda padded stickily across the kitchen lino, panting and displaying her long, pointed teeth. There was a quiet spell, waiting for the food to be ready, a strange quiet in which time distilled into a concentrate of anticipation, in which there was nothing to be said and nothing to be done but put utensils on the table and fill glasses — beer for Russell, tea for Muriel — and a bowl of water for Imelda.

—Okay, Rusty, tell me about Arlene. How come she dumped you?

   —It's not worth going into.

   —She met somebody else, right?

   —How did you know?

   —I didn't.

   —Well, yes, she did. End of story. I'm fine on my own.

   —Sure you are, Rusty.

   —Mmmmnnn. Great food. Is there any more?

   —Loads. I always cook for absent friends. Help yourself. I'm through playing housemaid.

   —D'you want some more?

   —No, no. Tiny people don't need too much to eat. And I like to leave a little space, so I'm not quite full, you know. To remember. To remember not having enough. When I was little, some neighbours had this big feast. All the food was laid out on a cloth decorated with rice and flower petals. My friends and I, we just stood and stared. We had never seen so much food and you know what? We could hardly eat anything. We were full up from just looking.

Russell took a smaller second helping than he really wanted. Muriel stared into the flames and her voice mellowed a fraction. Russell tried to chew quietly.

   —I am happy that you like my cooking. There's a scientific reason why chillies are good for sick hearts, Rusty.

—Pull the other one.

—Really. I'm talking endorphines. You know how people who don't do anything physical in their everyday life get hooked on puffing their guts out in gyms, how they get high from it? Well, chillies do the same thing, without all the effort.

—Is this some kind of oriental wisdom you're giving me?

—Dunno. I read it in *Elle*, or *Cosmo*.

Muriel sat down by the fire and wrapped her arms tightly across her chest. She had exchanged her battered donkey jacket for a bulky man's jersey which came down to her knees. The sleeves hung over her hands so that only the tips of her fingers were visible, tiny pink-nailed fingers, like a child's.

—I'm so cold! I never feel warm here. People from hot countries, our blood is thinner than yours.

—Is that a fact?

—Who knows. What's a fact after all? How can you believe in facts when our knowledge changes all the time?

—Well, thin blood or thick, you're hell of an exposed out here.

—I'm free here. I do what I want. Nobody sees, nobody knows.

Muriel grinned her disconcertingly wide grin, scooped up a shovelful of coal and threw it on the fire. In front of the hearth, Imelda was flattened out like a rug, snoozing, snoring and farting; her tail flapped against the floorboards in a jazzy, offbeat rhythm.

—So what d'you get up to that you're so secretive about?

—You know that really makes me mad. I say I want to be private and you think I've something to hide, some big dark secret.

—I'm just curious, that's all.

—You know what curiosity did.

Russell was beginning to feel weary; Muriel's combative style of conversation was wearing him down.

—I should phone for a taxi.

—Sorry, no phone. No telly, no radio, no phone. Peace and quiet, I told you. I do have an alarm clock in case I sleep in. But I never sleep in. Imelda makes sure of that.

—How will I get home?

—You need to get home?

—I don't suppose so.

—So stay here. Sleep on the couch. Look.

Muriel grabbed a loop of cloth neatly embedded in the seating and made a rapid assault on the settee. In a single agonised lurch, it contorted itself into a double bed. The batik sheets and quilt were held in place by a web of broad elastic straps with metal catches.

—I suppose there's not much choice.

—I could drop you at the end of the track. But you could wait all night there and not see a taxi.

—No phone there either, I suppose.

—Nope.

—What do you do out here if you've got a problem of some kind?

—I don't have problems. Not since my horrible hubby pissed off.

While Muriel splashed about in the bathroom, Russell turned off the over-head light and the room took on a cosy orange glow from the fire. He freed the blankets from their bonds, stripped off his outer clothes quickly – keeping on his socks and underwear – and snuggled up under the covers. When he heard Muriel emerging from the bathroom, he closed his eyes and lay still, pretending to be asleep; it seemed like the sensible thing to do.

—So.

—Hmm?

—Come on, Rusty, that's a lousy pretence.

—D'you want me to snore?

—God, no. Do you?

—So I'm told. Never noticed it myself.

—Ha ha. So.

Muriel stood in the doorway. She was still wearing her sweater but her legs were bare, smooth honey-coloured twigs poking out of a coarse wool sack.

—So?

—So how about some sex, Rusty?

—What?

—Don't you hear good? I said, sex. Screwing, fucking, banging, bonking, shagging, what you call it. What do you call it?

—Depends. But I mean . . . I hadn't . . . the thought hadn't . . . d'you really think it's a good idea?

—How do I know? It's not the kind of thing you can tell till you've tried it.

—No, but are you sure you want to? I mean, if it's all right with you . . . Christ, this is ridiculous.

—What's ridiculous?

—Talking like this. I mean we hardly know each other. You invited me for dinner. And you did insist that you weren't about to make a pass at me over the curry . . .

—I know what I said. I am not a forgetful person. I'm just now thinking your sick heart might begin to mend if someone took an interest in your body.

—That's very obliging of you, Muriel.

—No big deal. No big affair of the heart. I'm only talking about sex, Rusty. Safe sex, of course.

—Goes without saying but . . . but I don't know. I
suppose I wouldn't mind a bit of a cuddle.

—A bit of a cuddle! So that's what you call it.

Muriel screeched and giggled, threw off her sweater,
scrambled on to the creaking bed, and squirmed under the
covers.

She certainly didn't mess about. Russell had never met
a woman who required so little persuasion – none, in
fact. Or preamble. Or display of affection. Or suggestion
of interesting positions – she rapidly exhausted his tried
and tested angles and introduced him to some infinitely
more challenging ones. At a crucial moment, Imelda
woke up and added to the rumpus on the urgently wheez-
ing bed-settee by leaping in the air and trying to catch her
tail.

—How about a nightcap? said Muriel.

—I thought you didn't drink.

—Not before. After is okay. After I like to drink lots.
Before is stupid.

Russell had to admit that she had a point. Drink had all
too familiar drawbacks in that department, but it was the
usual way – drink, screw, sleep. Sleep would be nice now
but Muriel was wide awake and speedy as ever.

—Whisky?

—Twist my arm then. Just a wee one.

—Is that what you wanted?

—That's huge, Muriel.

—I don't mean the drink, dumbo. I mean the *cuddles*.

—I hadn't given it much thought.

—Huh.

—I don't mean . . . Christ, I mean, I'm not complain-
ing about . . . about getting . . . involved.

—Oh no, Rusty, we're not involved. And we're not going to get involved. I promise you.

—So all I'm good for is a one-night stand?

—Did I say that? Did I? Why don't you listen to what I say?

—Maybe we should try and sleep. It's late.

—Yeah yeah but I want to tell you a story.

—I'm not keen on stories, Muriel.

—Too bad. Put more coal on the fire, will you? And pass me my sweater.

—I'll warm you up.

—Gimme my goddamn sweater, Rusty.

Russell stoked the fire and got back under the covers. Muriel wriggled into the huge mud-coloured woolly, tucked her legs up inside it and wrapped her arms around her knees.

—Is this going to be a long story, Muriel?

—Wait and see. You don't have to listen. I talk to myself plenty out here, and to my dumb dog. Imelda the tyrant.

At the mention of her name, Imelda batted her tail against the floor. She was still splayed out in front of the fire, her thick, wavy coat toasting and exuding puffs of dog pong.

—Are you lying comfortably?

—Not really but go ahead.

—Okay okay. Once upon a time . . .

—You didn't say anything about it being a fairy tale.

—It's not. Once upon a time there was a girl born into a hut on stilts, where the land meets the sea. She was the result of a brief union between a poor woman and a marine biologist who stayed around long enough to name his baby Muriel. We don't name our babies properly straight away; the mortality rate is too high. We give them temporary names. Ugly names are the best: they show humility and keep the gods happy.

—You don't believe in all that.

—Why not?

—Well, microbiology and . . . animism don't seem to go together somehow.

—Huh. You people have one-line minds. So this girl survived, grew up and moved away from the coast and the constant threat of shifting tides and pirates. She moved from the village to the town, finally to the big city. Her departed daddy had done her one good turn, left money for her schooling and no matter how hard her poor mother tried to turn that fund into food, she couldn't. So this girl had white shirts and pleated navy skirts and even though her belly often burned with hunger, she did what her dear departed daddy planned – studied and studied, memorised lists of formulas for sugar, alcohol, salt, starch, amino acids. She grew blue jewels of copper sulphate and filled gas jars with stinky brown clouds of sulphur dioxide. Later, at college, she peered through microscopes and learned to recognise the pretty, plant-like molecular structures of spirochetes and other micro-organisms.

She found out that kids like her, who lived on the fringe of things – and her country being made up of seven thousand islands, there were a great many fringes – didn't usually get much schooling at all and college was out of the question. Worse still, so many children were dying from disease while people said the first lady owned 250 bras – including the bullet-proof variety – and over three thousand pairs of shoes. Though she had learnt to know and not know, see and not see, speak but say nothing, these things ate away at her. On the fringe of things where she had grown up, the margin between land and water, there were always secrets and from early on she could make her face go blank, her eyes opaque, she could become a closed book. But one evening, in Manila, sitting in the garden of her tutor, listening to other students talking – they talked quickly and quietly as always – part of a song flew through her head, so clear, like a bird in the bamboo:

> *Those who ask no questions,*
> *Won't be told no lies, so*
> *Watch the wall my darling*
> *While the gentlemen go by*

It was a song her daddy had sung to her, as a lullaby, when she was only two or three, before he decided that it was time for him to move on. Only later, much later, did she understand the real meaning of the words.

—Where do you think your old man went?

—Another sea, another shack. Back to Burntisland. Who knows?

—Burntisland! Is that why you came to Scotland? To track down your old man?

—No.

—Quite a coincidence, then.

—Yes.

—You don't want to talk about it.

—No. Not now.

—Fair enough. Burntisland, of all places. So you're half Scottish then?

—Mixed blood, Rusty, has nothing to do with who or what I am.

He should sleep, he must sleep. Muriel had bustled off to her bedroom, dragging Imelda with her:

—I feel much more secure with a dog in my bed than a man.

Well, that was that and he wasn't going to make a fuss about it. Apart from the occasional crackle and flare from the fire, there was no noise to speak of, no noise to bother him. And yet the quiet itself held his attention, kept him listening for something to disturb it. But nothing did, except his own body shifting on the pull-out bed.

He would have liked the morning's drama to have meant more. If Arlene's author had got a hold of that little episode, he'd have made it as crummy and inconsequential as every other detail of Russell's life that he'd appropriated from Arlene. But it was bloody something, rescuing a half-dead night watchman from Antarctica as your first task of the day. Days like today didn't often happen in real life: they happened on telly, in novels, days when unexpected and possibly catastrophic events piled on a character, transforming a life forever, or at least until the next episode.

Would Muriel be in the next episode? He wasn't at all sure that he wanted her there. It wasn't the time to be getting mixed up with another woman, a woman with a husband somewhere, a husband who finds a gap in the market, any market as long as it pays, and tries to fill it. Muriel had seemed glad enough that her husband had skedaddled but still angry with him for something else. When she'd spoken of him, she'd tossed her head as if she were trying to shake something out of her hair.

Mixed blood . . . hot blood, cold blood, new blood, blue blood, heart's blood, whole blood. Blood stock, blood lust, blood sports, blood pressure, blood stream, bloodstone, bloodshot, blood sample, blood count, blood brother, blood hunt, blood cell, blood stain, blood money, blood bank, blood shed . . .

FIFTEEN

How I See Myself

Eating Passionfruit in Bed: the sexiest book you'll read this year!

Not just a single copy but half a wall of them. Russell fixed his incensed gaze on the reassuringly innocuous cover of a book about vets; a sketchy water-colour illustration of a veteran Ford chugging along a winding country road. If *Passionfruit* – the perfect stocking-filler for randy readers – was in the hospital shop, it must be everywhere: in airports, stations, maybe even in supermarkets – the title would go down well in supermarkets, they might even do a special promotion – a free pound of fruit with every copy . . .

—Excuse me, sir. If ye dinnae quit it I'm gonnae havetae call security.

The young female shop assistant poked his arm.

—Can ye stop chuckin they books around, sir. The

covers'll get all crushed and bent and naebody'll want tae buy them.

He'd cleaned out the whole display case. Copies of *Passionfruit* now lay embedded in trays of marshmallows and crisps. The aisle was awash with laminated gobbets of green and orange pulp.

—Are ye no well?

—I'm fine. It . . . it was an accident.

—I thought maybe you were having a wee turn.

—I'm not a patient, I'm a visitor! Do I look like a patient? Am I wearing pyjamas?

—We get a lot of day patients, sir. Day patients dinnae wear pyjamas. For the psychiatric unit mostly.

The girl bent down to retrieve the books.

—Were you wanting a copy, sir?

Russell didn't wait for his change from the bumper joke book and the jar of mixed nuts. Following the arrows to the wards, he turned into a corridor. A huge mural accosted him. A hundred novice artists – from tots to grannies – had responded with paintbrushes and varying degrees of talent to the title *How I See Myself*. A hundred self-portraits from the most elementary daubs to painstaking likenesses jostled for attention.

The corridor was long, low-ceilinged and stuffy. The walls were covered with more murals which alternated between garish abstracts and idealised depictions of honest labour in traditional and mostly obsolete skills: black-faced miners hewing coal, a ruddy crofter prodding a bullock-driven plough across a half-tilled field, colonies of ant-size shipbuilders engaged in useful activity in the cross-section of a massive ocean-going vessel. It all added up to a potted history of an economy and a way of life which had been systematically eroded during the span of his own lifetime. Even the oil-rig-by-sunset scene looked quaint, historical, irrelevant.

Maximum two visitors per patient. Bobby was at the far end of the small ward. In a decrepit dressing gown and chewed-looking slippers, he lay on his bed, facing the wall. Other patients had one or two visitors, other bedsides hummed with subdued, solicitous conversation, other tables were quietly cheery with floral sprays, GET WELL cards, fruit, soft drinks. Bobby's held a plastic jug of water and a handful of screwed-up sweetie papers.

—Not much of a view, Bobby.

Bobby turned slowly.

—Ken. Boring as fuck. Still, it's restful. At least ah dinnae havetae stare at that art they've got in the corridors. A blank wa's fine by me. Good of you to come, by the way.

—How're you doing?

—Dying for a smoke.

—You're allowed to smoke?

—No really: cos of ma wee stroke, ken. But there's a smoke room and auld habits die hard. Waste bin in there's stowed out wi dowts by the end of the day. Hell of a lot of smokers in this place. Got any cigs?

—Sorry. Chucked it years ago.

—You'd take it up again if ye were in here. Bugger all else tae dae but smoke, ken.

Bobby laughed but the laugh broke into a hacking cough. His hands were bandaged. Otherwise he looked much as he'd done before the accident: scrawny, hollow about the eyes, fissured cheeks.

—Apart from no tobacco, how are you?

—Done in, man.

—Had any visitors?

—Have ah no, Fairley. Doctors, polis, press. The fucking inquisition.

Another coughing fit caught Bobby short. He sank back on the bed and looked up at the ceiling.

—Too many fags, man. Ah should thank you, Fairley.

—Forget it. I owed you one, anyway.

—How d'ye mean?

—The freeze-dryer, remember – the buggered freeze-dryer?

Russell had been on call. One weekend a month he took a turn along with some other maintenance boys. Well, you took these things seriously for a while, but when you've sat at home, being responsible for ages and there's not so much as a crackle from the intercom, you begin to think it's never going to happen and then you discover that your girlfriend has fucked off for good and you drag out the remains of the CD collection and trawl through it, cursing Arlene and listening to footsteps passing by on the street, always passing by as you drown in self-pity. The hours slosh away until all you're fit for is to crawl to bed and the bloody bleeper starts up. You ignore it for a while. Sometimes it just goes off by itself for no reason. There's never been a real reason yet, never a single bona fide call-out but the bleeper doesn't stop, so you tune in and Bobby's on the intercom, jabbering on about the freeze-dryer making the wrong noises. It's 2.45 a.m. and you're in no state to go anywhere.

—Ah'm no happy about this, Fairley. Ah'm no covered for operating machinery.

—I'll talk you through it. It'll be fine.

Thank Christ Bobby'd been on form that night. Though

Russell had identified the problem, dealing with it demanded a steady hand and total concentration, not a barrage of contradictory emotions.

—Ah've no thought aboot it.

—You were a godsend that night . . .

—Ach, well, ma halo's no shinin the now, Fairley.

Bobby held up his bandaged hands.

—Only two fingers tae frostbite. Bloody lucky, ah'm tellt.

Russell laid the joke book on the bed.

—There might be a laugh or two in there for you.

Bobby grinned at the cover cartoon.

—Ta. It'll be a laugh trying tae turn the pages.

—So, are they looking after you?

—Some no bad wee nurses, right enough. The one that does the bed baths is a soor coo but the night nurse is a cracker. Wheels in the drugs trolley just like she's an air hostess doin the duty free. Nice uniform tae; tight fittin. Black stockings. No many huv the black stockings the now, mair's the pity. White leather shoes creaking on the lino . . . The lights are doon and it's dead still and quiet – apart frae the moans and groans, ken – and then you see her, comin in frae the corridor, aw bleached and tanned, in the wee white suit.

—Isn't that what nurses look like after medication?

Bobby's head sank back against his pillow. The joke book slid from his bandaged hands on to the threadbare, over-laundered bedcover. His eyes closed.

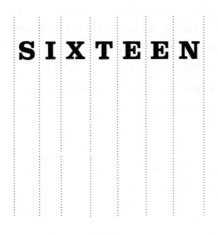

SIXTEEN

Blood Orange

The key wouldn't fit into the lock because there was another one on the inside. Russell rang the bell and hammered on the door.

—Open up, Arlene. Open this bloody door.

No response. He hammered again, then pushed open the letter box and peered inside. The lights were on but there was no sign of anyone. He put his mouth to the letter box and roared:

—You've gone too far, Arlene, too fucking far. Let me in!

What was worse than being stuck outside your own home, unable to get in? It was cold and dark and the few folk going by were casting suspicious glances at him as if he were a potential burglar and not a paid-up resident of the flat to which he was unable to gain entry. Even old Mrs Slater, from two doors down, tutted as she hirpled along to the post box, a hand clutching her cut-glass brooch as if he might chase after her and rip it off her coat. Christ, he'd been saying hello to her for years, done her shopping when she had the shingles, even she was against him now that he was stuck outside his own door.

Sonia and Parveen flapped their skipping ropes along the street and stopped at his gate.

—Hiya, Mr Fairley.

—Arlene was here a wee while ago.

—She's gone away now.

—I was going to say that. Why do you always have to say what I'm just going to say?

—She had a big boy with her.

—It wasn't a boy. It was a man. She had a man with her, Mr Fairley.

—Really. Terrific.

—Why don't we ever see Arlene, Mr Fairley?

—We saw her today, stupid.

—What you say is what you are, so you're stupid.

—Thanks for the information, girls.

Sonia drew herself up proudly, tossed her long pigtails over her shoulders and skipped seriously along the pavement. Parveen flashed him a smile, puckered her brows and charged after her sister:

—Wait for me! I hate you! You never wait for me!

A man. Arlene had left a man in the flat. Fox? F.B. Fox rooting around, taking notes for future reference: *how the dumped lover lives*, observing the habitat at close quarters? It was all there: the dust, the grime, the empty bottles, crushed cans, festering takeaway remains, a week's dirty clothes spilling out of the laundry basket, a tide mark of stubble ringing the sink like iron filings, the stale, pervasive stink of neglect.

He began to kick the door, knowing it was pointless. A heavy door with a double mortice, he'd break his foot before he broke in but he continued kicking all the same. The lock clicked. Twice. The door opened, slowly. Lag, Arlene's dishwasher, smiled moistly. His personal stereo was clipped to a heavy, studded belt slung round skinny hips. Headphones bobbed against his collarbone.

—Hiya. Didn't hear you. Come on in.

—What's going on?

—You want to come in and shut the door? It's cold out there.

—I know it's fucking cold. I was standing there long enough.

—Want a cup of tea? said Lag.

—A cup of tea? Listen, son, if I want a cup of tea, I'll make myself one, right? I live here, for Christ's sake.

—I'm not using your tea bags, Mr Fairley. Arlene brought me some supplies. You planning on a night out?

—What's that supposed to mean?

—Just like, well it might be a good idea.

Lag opened the living-room door. Furniture had been piled in the centre of the floor and covered with dust sheets. The carpet was covered in torn strips of wallpaper. The room reeked of dope.

—I'm kind of in the middle of things here.

Lag grinned again, a vacant, enraging grin. Russell grabbed him by his torn overalls and shoved him up against a soggy, half-stripped wall.

—WHAT IS GOING ON?

—Easy, Mr Fairley, easy, eh. Arlene said to let myself in and get on with it. Said she'd cleared it with you, man.

Lag's eyes and mouth had opened wide and remained that way, a mixture of disbelief and the kind of wary acquiescence you'd give a deranged, violent assailant.

—Bitch. Lying, cheating, self-centred, cold-blooded bitch.

Russell was aware that his repertoire of insults was pitifully limited but at that moment he couldn't think of anything worse to call Arlene.

—So, like, you're saying it isn't cool?

Russell loosened his grip on Lag's limp shoulders: Lag unstuck his head from the wall.

—Christ, none of this is your fault.

—The kitchen's okay, said Lag. I haven't started in there yet. Sure you don't want a cup of tea?

—I was thinking more along the lines of several pints in rapid succession, followed by several whiskies.

—You want to watch it with the booze, man.

—You want to watch it with the wacky baccy. What a stink.

—Sorry. Gets me focused. It's cool when a whole strip of paper comes off in a oner. But some are like totally stubborn, like they don't want to leave the wall, like they're trying to tell you it's lives you're pulling away.

—Must take a hell of a time to strip a wall, if that's what you're thinking while you're doing it.

—D'you think houses have spirits?

—Other than the kind kept in bottles, no.

—I don't mean ghosts or anything, but, like, essences.

—If you start thinking the wallpaper's got a soul, Christ . . .

—Thinking about getting a blowtorch. Speed things up.

—No fucking way. A couple of joints and you'd be blasting the furniture instead of the walls.

Lag scratched his head. Flakes of sodden wallpaper fell out of his hair.

—Hash doesn't make you feel like that. Didn't you ever try it, man, back in the sixties?

—The seventies, man, the late seventies! Once or twice, after too many pints. Made me throw up.

—Yeah, well, it can do.

The few times Russell had tried cannabis had been disasters. He had no real interest in the drug itself. It was the talent that hung around the joint rollers he'd been taken by: arts students mostly, panda-eyed lassies in see-through tops and crotch-hugging jeans, who spent most of their time in a stoned haze. He'd fancied a couple of them, Patti and Val, from Moral Philosophy 1. *You take care of the morals, I'll take care of the biochemistry* had been his chat-up line but Patti and Val had drifted off in the direction of a couple of whey-faced posers who burbled on about existentialism, free love and art for art's sake through a fug of dope smoke. Back in the seventies.

Lag took his joint from the ashtray.

—Is it cool?

—On you go. Could be worse, I suppose . . . Got enough work these days?

—Six nights at Boon's, Sunday lunch at The Monsoon, three or four dawn-patrol shifts at The Blood Orange.

—All dish washing?

—My speciality. Dishes are dishes. The hands get fucked but I've got a good cream now, a herbal remedy, not tested on animals, I don't like that animal testing, that guinea pig shit.

Lag's hands were red raw, a startling contrast to the never-seen-the-light-of-day pallor of his forearms and face.

Russell followed Lag to the kitchen. Using Arlene's tea bags, he made a pot of tea and rinsed out a couple of mugs. He had to. They were all dirty. Lag eyed the sink sagely.

—I'm the same, man. Anybody else's dishes and I'm right in there with the sleeves rolled up. But my own, I let them lie. Barb gets pissed off about it but, like, you can only wash so many dishes.

—Still with Barbara, then?

—Yeah. On we go . . .

—How long is it now?

—Seven years. Since we were fifteen. A long time.

Outside, the reverberating thud of something heavy smashing against something solid was followed by the unmistakable skittering of broken glass. Russell went to the window and looked out, expecting to see a car wrapped around a lamppost. He saw a sofa and a kitchen cabinet. On the first floor across the street, the Union Jack blind had been pulled up and the new neighbours were hanging out of the window, admiring their efforts. Jagged shards from the smashed windows of the cabinet had come to rest on the sofa. Under the beam of the streetlight, they glinted viciously.

—Take a look at this, said Russell.

Lag glanced at the furniture on the street and the open window then turned away faster than Russell had ever seen him move.

—Can you close the curtains, Mr Fairley? Can you do it right now? said Lag, his back to the street.

—D'you know that pair?

—As much as I want to.

S E V E N T E E N

Star-Spangled Tipi

—Spare change?

Driving sleet blew into Russell's face and slush sprayed up from the wheels of buses and lorries. Hordes of late-night shoppers laden with awkward boxes and wayward bags swayed stolidly along the pavement like panniered mules. The windows of travel agents were plastered with sunburn-coloured fliers offering cut-price winter breaks: in Lanzarote, Tenerife, Barbados, Dominica, Goa, The Gambia; there was no shortage of places where the sun was shining ferociously, the sky was unbroken blue and the sand stretched miles beyond the edge of the brochure photograph.

Beggars huddled under damp blankets, old folks in thin coats pegged along stiffly, toddlers with blue legs and blazing faces wailed as their parents yanked them along the pavement. Seasonal cheer, Christ, suffering humanity. Even the charity collectors, rattling cans on every block, looked chilled and miserable, their hands red raw, throats hoarse from exhorting the passing population to consider those less fortunate than themselves.

The big stores had already tarted up their windows with tinsel and reindeer, and premature sleigh bell music skittered through briefly-opened doors. The central bookshop had devoted an entire window to the collected works of Franklin B. Fox, a pyramid of passionfruit pulp in the foreground and a sheaf of publicity posters; more pulp, magnified. *The Free Lunch* and other earlier titles fanned across the black backdrop. All of them, Russell noticed, contained some mention of food. Was that it? Had a common interest in food been the real attraction? Dream on, son.

—Spare change?

Russell handed a pocketful of coins to the next beggar he passed: *there but for fortune* . . . The young man's reedy thanks was whipped away by the wind. The way things were looking, fortune – in the guise of Arlene – was nudging him in a similar direction. He'd have to look for somewhere else to live, soon, very soon. But not yet. House-hunting could bloody well wait. It was payday and he was going shopping.

There was something numbing about the cavernous clothing store, a muffled, airless hangar of winter-weight wool and polyester in navy, charcoal, brown, black.

—Need any help?

—Just looking.

—I'll leave you to it then.

The salesman, a spotty kid in a stiff, three-piece suit, frowned and resumed doing nothing.

The overhead lighting in the changing room was harsh

and unflattering. And the jeans he was wearing – bagging at the bum and concertinaed at the ankles, didn't do a thing for any of the jackets he tried on. New jeans would be good, a shirt, too, for that matter, a jersey, socks, underwear. Footwear. A pair of thick-soled boots or Cuban heels would give him a bit of extra height but no, the jacket would have to do. After an age of working his arms in and out of sleeves, and considering price tags in relation to his bank balance, he eventually made a purchase.

The pub was deserted, but warm enough to order a pint and sit by the gas flames and plastic logs. Some clever clogs had thrown fag ends on the fake fire; they lay piled in little ashy cairns, unconsumed. A good pint, all the same. A bloody good pint.

—Want a look at the newspaper?

—Yeah . . . no . . . I'll skip the paper.

The barman's smooth round face had a heavy blue shadow along the jaw. He was a big bloke, full-bodied in a reassuring, wholesome sort of way. Reassuring, wholesome and bald. Why couldn't Fox have written in a baldie like that, instead of greasy, peelie-wally Leslie Little?

—Quite right. Sometimes you just don't want to know what's going on in the world, do you? I've enough to be going on with in here. When the door opens you just never know what's going to blow in off the street. This time of day, it's usually not too bad, still . . .

The place wasn't exactly heaving with rowdies. Russell and a handful of old codgers in the corner, hunched over whisky chasers and a cutthroat game of dominoes, could hardly qualify as trouble.

—When it's quiet like this you can be caught off guard. Want the telly on?

—No thanks.

—Something to eat? Steak pie? Chilli? The chilli will plunge into places other foods fear to go. Or there's chicken and chips.

—Maybe later.

No point in hurrying home.

—Been treating yourself?

The new jacket lay on the bench beside him, straining the seams of its plastic carrier.

—Let's have a look. Nothing worse than a bad buy.

—I've paid for it, it'll have to do.

—Always get a second opinion. You don't want to spend months coveting every other jacket you see . . . well, don't say I didn't warn you.

Russell concentrated on his pint. The barman went back to keeping himself busy. The door opened and a funnel of wind shot across the floor. The beggar from outside the bookshop blew in on its tail.

—Ach, Christ, man. No heat in this, he said, thrusting his hands closer to the flames. Virtual reality, man, that's what this is. Flames, logs, but no heat. Jee zuzz . . . oh it's you, he said. Hiya. I always remember a face. Ta for the tap. A shudder racked his whole body. He pushed his hands further into the fake fire.

—This flaming coat, man, this coat has seen better days. Russell could smell him; a sharp reek of the street came off him in gusts. His voice was cracked and harsh but his handshake was weak, pitifully weak.

—Peter's the name by the way. That one won't serve me, I can tell.

—Your money's as good as the next man's.

Peter was right about the barman but knew somewhere

that might be worth a try. The Oasis was an unqualified hole: greasy yellow lights, furred flock wallpaper, plastic seats pocked with burn holes, the smell of full ashtrays, spilt beer. It was two small rooms knocked into a long, thin one by means of an archway. In the back made no cosier by the addition of a gilt-framed mirror and a tub of dusty plastic roses, a folk duo picked guitars and moaned the Skye Boat Song; their audience was in a state of communal catatonic gloom.

As Russell waited for his order, a woman elbowed past him and pounded her fists on the bar.

—Where's ma whiskies? What have you done wi ma whiskies?

Her bottle-black hair had two fingers of grey at the parting. Lipstick overran the ragged contours of her pinched mouth.

—I'm asking you a question, lady, she said.

—You drank them, said the barmaid.

—I what? I what? Bloody stinking little liar.

—It's the truth. You drank both of them.

—Lying bitch. A sin so it is. Cheating a poor woman out of her money. A fucking sin.

The young barmaid shook her head and continued pouring two pints of heavy.

—AH WANT MA WHISKY. GIMME MA WHISKY, YA DIRTY, THIEVIN COW!

As the bouncer, thick-set, square-jawed, humourless, appeared from the back room there was a buzz of fuddled apprehension. He strode to the bar and slapped down a couple of pound coins. What began as a hushed exchange rapidly drowned out the hired guitars.

—Take the fucking money AND LEAVE!

—AH DON'T WANT MA MONEY. AH WANT MA

WHISKY. CALL THE POLIS. SOMEBODY CALL THE POLIS. AH WANT JUSTICE, JUSTICE!

The woman picked up the coins, lobbed them across the room then lunged at the bouncer, grabbing his shirt. Until then, the sour-faced thug had been restraining himself but when the woman started tearing at his clothes, messing up his image, he lost it, wrenched her hands off his shirt, shoved them behind her back and dragged her towards a table.

—Stupid old cow, he hissed. This your wife?

A thin, greasy-haired man nodded vaguely, distantly and gazed at the flock wallpaper as if he were engrossed in an absorbing inner movie.

—Get her out of here, or I will!

The woman roared, lashed out and flailed with all her skinny, drunken might, twirled out of the bouncer's grasp and crashed to the floor. The bouncer grabbed her ankles, kicked her hands off the table leg she was gripping and dragged her, feet first to the exit.

The bouncer's rage at being pawed by a customer paralysed the room. Until the woman hit the street – and the thud could be heard through double doors – nobody moved. After a brief, potent silence Peter sprang out of his seat and went to see what was going on outside. The man who had – under pressure – admitted to being the woman's husband, also tagged along, with less enthusiasm. In spite of the melancholic strains from the back, the customers in the front room were hushed, the flush of complicity on every woozy face, as if they'd let one take the blame for all. Heads turned fractionally in the direction of the window at the sound of a heavy object hitting it persistently. Russell downed his drink and left.

Outside, the woman was hurling herself at the pub

window with no sense of self-preservation. Her husband was pointing a tobacco-brown finger at the scowling, adamant bouncer. Peter was prancing between the pair of them like a referee. None of the men paid any attention to the woman until a taxi crept up the slushy street and – when the bouncer hailed it – miraculously stopped. Without any visible emotion, the woman's husband picked her off the street and piled her inside.

—You're fucking barred, the bouncer bawled as the taxi moved off, slush spraying from its wheels and spattering his crisp black chinos.

Peter walked fast and talked fast.

—I want all of it, man. I want what you've got. Your house, your job, your jacket. I want a life. Anybody's'll do, except mine. Trade you. I get the house, the job, the bird – I want a bird, Christ, I'd take the bird and forget the rest. Got a bird?

—Not really. But what's in this for me?

—You?

Peter grinned, revealing more gaps than teeth. He was too young for such a desolate mouth.

—You'd get the freedom of the city, man. The capital by night, that's what, world famous views, the spectacular fucking capital skyline.

At the top of the Playfair Steps, they stopped and looked down at the city lights sweeping all the way down to the firth. The new jacket was bloody freezing. Peter was wearing Russell's old fleece over his own manky raincoat. Even in his current state of beery magnanimity, that was as much of a trade-off as Russell would go along with. The sleet had given way to large, loose snowflakes which drifted towards the slushy puddles underfoot.

—Nice, the lights, eh, the reds and yellows? It's like getting a wee heat looking at the lights, if you're in the mood to see it like that. Not that my imagination's usually so cheery. See down the brae, all those houses, all those homes? There's a room down there. I might take it, I might. He pulled a squashed fag packet from his coat. It had an address written on the lid.

—See? I'm to go there and see about a room.

Beside them, at the top of the steps, pegged down with guy ropes, the recently erected Christmas tree swayed gently, like a star-spangled tipi.

EIGHTEEN

Blood Groups

By coffee time the works' cafeteria was buzzing. Above each table, a resonant hum hung in the air. Newspapers were being passed around, handed from one table to another, even rolled up and tossed across the room, open at the pages where the story of Bobby's time in the deep-freeze had been reported, under headlines like **NIGHT MAN'S DEEP FREEZE ORDEAL** and **CHILLED-OUT WATCHMAN'S MIRACLE ESCAPE.**

Bobby had been lucky, right enough. He'd noticed from the close-circuit TV that the red light was flashing in the deep freeze, had gone to investigate, suffered a minor stroke and a fall in the process. Though he'd lost two fingers to frostbite, the man had got off very lightly, considering. It came down to timing. He'd passed out around seven a.m. Russell had found him just after nine. An hour or two more in Antarctica and the cold would have done for him, even though, as the power had been off, the deep freeze would have been getting relatively warmer by the minute.

As well as photos of Bobby holding up his bandaged hands and quotes from him on what it felt like to have cheated death, Everett had been grilled about various aspects of work at the plant. He'd outlined the plant's extensive safety procedures and emphasised its motto for dealing with any questionable batch of products: *if in doubt, throw it out.* Nevertheless, each and every article had aimed to plant seeds of unease in its readers.

Muriel lit a cigarette and leaned towards Russell.

—I think they should have said more about your act of bravery. You did risk your own health. Think about it. Recovering from a virus then being exposed to extreme cold like that couldn't have done your immune system any good.

—There's no story in my immune system.

True, his own part in the drama had barely been mentioned: *pulled to safety by a fellow worker* was about the extent of it. But given his recent personal experience of the printed word Russell was relieved, even grateful to the papers for virtually ignoring him.

—I went to see Bobby the other day.

—How was he?

—Not bad. Not so good. A bit edgy, sort of nervously chatty, rabbiting on about anything and everything. Like the night nurse. He's got the hots for his night nurse. Not at all bad, if it was the one I saw coming on duty.

—Excuse me?

—The night nurse.

—I hear you, Rusty, but why are you telling me this?

—Because you asked me about Bobby.

—Did I ask you about the night nurse?

—I'm just filling you in on Bobby's present state of play, seeing as you asked.

—I asked about the man's health, goddamn it, not his cock-a-doodle.

Muriel spluttered a ragged plume of smoke into his face then hid her grin behind her sleeve. Everett was bustling down the glass-walled passage towards the cafeteria. When he reached the open door, he stopped. Conversation plummeted then resumed at a more subdued level. Papers were surreptitiously closed, folded, rolled-up, stuck in pockets. The man just stood there, hands jutting stiffly from his cuffs, jacket unbuttoned, tie slithering down the front of his shirt. Everett had never been known as a sharp dresser but this morning he was a shambles. As he cast a fretful eye across the crowded tables, his lips moved in a damp, insanitary sort of way. He was looking for someone.

—Sorry to cut short your break, Fairley.

Todd was already in Everett's office, spreading printouts across the desk like battle plans; several had ominous red circles around temperature clusters. Everett cleared his throat and flopped into his chair. The requirements of a sterile environment had promoted hi-tech design features – in management quarters at any rate – and the stream-lined furniture emphasised Everett's disarray. Todd seemed intent on a space midway between Everett's crumpled sleeve and the stainless steel desk.

—Please acquaint yourself with these sample printouts taken over the last six months.

Russell made a futile attempt to study the endless columns of figures in front of him but they kept sliding out of alignment, twisting and turning in a jumping blur of grey and pink stains. The room was warm and smelled of Todd's musky cologne, the acrid cleaning fluid and sweat; it was not an invigorating combination. Outside, a heavy, churning sky pressed down on the landscaped driveway and the test-tube Madonna.

—Nasty day, said Everett.

—It is that.

—Nasty world out there too, nasty bloody-minded world. Some people think that we came into the world innocent, Fairley. I used to think that myself but I'm coming round to the idea of original sin, do you know what I'm saying?

—I'm not sure that I do

—Never mind, never mind . . . I'm sure I don't need to spell out what these figures indicate.

A lot of extra work for a start.

The wind slapped a sapling against the window. A sleek dark blue Volvo turned into the visitors' parking area and pulled up. Two men – dark suits, discreet ties – and a tall, blonde woman lowered their heads and made their way to the visitors' entrance. The wind whipped the woman's hair across her face and ballooned her skirt. She fought to keep the skirt under control but the skirt rebelled. Germaine Shuck looked more or less the same – though her hair was loose rather than braided; a bad choice considering the weather. Russell's skin raged. His tongue rasped against the roof of his mouth like a loofah. Jesus fucking Christ. Ask Todd to recommend a good lawyer and, in a city hoaching with members of the legal profession, he puts you on to the works' firm. It was too hot, far too hot in Everett's office. Chairs grazed the marble-effect linoleum. Briefcases were clicked open and snapped shut. There was a crackle of static as Ms Shuck crossed her legs. Everett's burbling introductions were faint, muffled. By staying very still Russell was willing himself to become invisible.

His name was mentioned; heads nodded, teeth were bared briefly but the attention of the triumvirate rapidly returned to Everett and Todd. It was Everett they were here to see, after all. And Todd was better-looking, younger, held a superior position and wore a suit. To the representatives of Anglesey and Hope he was just a bloke in overalls. But didn't Ms Shuck remember him? Was he really so insignificant? Could lady luck, for once, be on his side?

The pressure off for the moment, Russell began to relax enough to look up from the sickening swarm of figures on the table. Everett was banging on about Bobby's misadventures in Antarctica. He was talking too fast and too much. Strings of saliva hung from the corners of his mouth; he tried to flick them away with his tongue but this only seemed to add to the general precipitation. Though the men were nodding sagely, Ms Shuck seemed to have trouble focusing her attention on Everett. For all his recent enthusiasm for oriental women, Todd had a long-standing weakness for blondes. Even today, he'd switched to allure mode, and was making persistent eye contact with Ms Shuck.

Keep it up, son, keep it up.

— . . . and it was Mr Fairley, here, who was present at the . . . scene of the, eh, incident.

Ms Shuck's upper body swung towards Russell. Her elbows relocated themselves on the table. Her lips parted. Her lipstick was the same fire-engine red as when he'd sat in her wood-panelled office and poured out his personal woes. Perhaps she always wore the same shade. Her smooth forehead crinkled into a sympathetic frown.

—It must have been a traumatic experience for you, Mr . . .

—FAIRLEY.

The bugger shouted it. Why did Everett have to shout his name?

—Yes, of course. Sorry, I'm hopeless with names. So many people pass through our practice every day, you know, that I've just given up on names. At least until they become long-term clients, that is.

—It's a *fairly* common name, said Todd, his voice syrupy. Unlike yours.

—Fairley. Does ring a bell, though. Never mind, it will come to me later. So you were the hero of the day, then? Single-handed, you dragged this unfortunate man to safety?

—Didn't have any choice.

—Oh, I don't know, you could have panicked and run away and by the time you got back, the poor man might have been dead. People often think they don't have a choice when really they do, but sometimes they've already made the choice before a situation occurs, do you know what I mean? You see, somebody like you – a brave man – probably made the choice much earlier in your life about what you felt you *should* do *in the event of* such a situation occurring. I don't mean that you had a crystal ball and could see a man lying unconscious in a deep freeze, I don't mean anything like that, it's more of a *general attitude*, a *leaning towards* selfless behaviour. Dear me, I do go on, don't I? You can probably tell I'd have preferred criminal law to corporate.

Her partners at Anglesey and Hope grumbled their agreement.

—Yes, well, if Mr Fairley might just relate – briefly – the circumstances under which he found the night watchman, said Everett, and then return to his duties . . .

—Of course, she said. I'm all ears.

Even after a couple of tellings, Russell had begun to embellish the facts of his rescue operation with atmospheric detail but for now he pared it down to the barest, driest of bones and got the hell out of Everett's office.

NINETEEN

Close

It had been weeks, no months, since Russell had been behind a wheel and he was itching to get shot of the city and put his foot down. The traffic had thinned out and the streets by night looked desolate. A thickset man dragged a dog along the pavement, its heavy coat swinging as it lumbered after its master. A gang of teenagers huddled in the remains of a bus shelter. The glass had been smashed out leaving a metal frame. Behind it, the sparsely lit windows of the highrises were the only source of light, the highrises which shook when the wind blew, harboured damp, deprivation, asthma and addiction. Bugger all to do but hang about inside a clapped-out bus shelter, playing chicken with passing traffic, waiting for life to begin. If it wasn't over already. In the mornings, on his way to work, he'd see the local kids plodding towards the school, hunched against the world and the limited prospects it had to offer.

At the roundabout he took the right fork. Heading for the hills again. Even if he wouldn't be climbing them tonight, even if he wouldn't even be seeing them, it was good to know they were there, long fingers of rock pointing south and west. One thing he liked about the city was how little time it took to get out of it. The change was sudden, dramatic: one minute you were in the concrete zone, the next you were passing stone cottages and revamped coach houses, with olde-worlde carriage lamps and floodlit millstones.

The road was quiet; most of the traffic had filtered off elsewhere at the roundabout. Nobody up ahead, nobody on his tail, the occasional blast of oncoming headlights but otherwise he was cocooned in the beam of his own on a road like a licorice whip with cats' eyes starring the bends. No need to think about anything except that it wouldn't be a good idea to take the next bend as fast as the last one. Speed was so deceptive. When you first accelerated you felt it but you got used to it so quickly and it didn't seem fast at all. Until you hit the next bend.

The car was dirty. Filthy. Arlene had turned it into a dustbin. Plenty petrol, though. And this week's *Property Guide* with Arlene's scrawl across the top of the front page: *I've hired a van. It's costing me a fortune. Please don't make it a total waste of money.* Bugger that. No way was he going house-hunting. He switched on the radio, tried to find some decent music but the hills interfered with the reception; all he could pick up clearly was a growling church organ and a smooth, female voice. He opted for the voice.

If you lived in New York all your life, you might never know a place like this existed, right at the very heart of it all. A stone's throw from the grey tundra-like landscape of the Hudson, a few blocks from the dayglo buns and bottled impossibles of Chinatown, there's a little old cottage which could have been taken from Cork or Donegal and dropped here.

—*Somebody did that,* a male voice replied. *Stone by stone. I admire that dedication, don't you? Can I fix you some coffee? It's all I have. I live simply, as you see. I buy things and then they run out so I buy them again. I write a story, then I run out of ideas, so I write another. One thing at a time. One plot at a time, one jug of coffee. It's Brazilian; a nice kick to it. Sure you won't?*

Christ, said Russell, a fucking writer.

—*And what about women,* said the woman. *Is it one woman at a time?*

—*Sure,* said the writer. *I'm a serial monogamist. I may be many things – people have called me many things, most of which say more about them than me, of course – but greedy I'm not. I find one woman, man, one animal, I mean, animals can be very deep don't you think? – One creature at a time is enough to be going on with.*

—*Your latest novel,* said the woman . . . *The blurb claims that it's the last literary word on sexual relations.*

—*Well, hey, they have to say something on the jacket,* said the writer.

—*A three-hundred-page ejaculation, was how someone described it,* said the woman. *I wonder how you, personally, feel about this book, indeed all your books being described as a stream of semen?*

—*Did somebody say that? Are you allowed to say that on radio?*

—*I don't know but yes, somebody did say that. I did.*

—*Jeez,* said the writer, *you had me worried. I thought you'd seen it in print somewhere. It's a really gross expression. I may be old-fashioned but I hate to hear dirty words from the mouth of a pretty woman. Or from her pen. I wouldn't print that, Miss, if I were you. Let me tell you something. This book may look as if it's about sex because that's the action, see? But you don't say a Shakespeare play's about killing just because it ends with bodies all over the stage, do you? That's just the surface detail. The book is about identity, gender, the hidden agenda, about a level of existence which goes beyond social mores, beyond morality. Basically, it's about passion.*

—Could you elaborate on that? said the woman.

—Well, no I couldn't. It's in the goddamn book. I only write the stuff. I don't know what it means.

—You mean you don't have any control over what you write?

—No, not exactly. But I have no control over other people's interpretations. And other people's hangups. You see, when you read my book and see only bodily functions, that says more about you than me.

—But isn't it the case, said the woman, *that a reader can only find something that's there, even if the writer wasn't aware of putting it in?*

—God knows. I'm just a humble practitioner of my craft, like the guys that drive these boats up and down the river. Mostly they get it right but, once in a long while, they miscalculate and go off course. Do you have any idea how many vessels use this waterway?

—No, said the woman.

—Neither do I, said the writer.

— . . .

— . . .

—Well, thank you for that illuminating insight into your work and your philosophy.

You have been listening to: FROM THE FOXHOLE: *an interview with acclaimed author Franklin B. Fox, whose latest novel,* Eating Passionfruit . . .

As Russell took another corner, the oncoming beam of a bus swung into his eyes, dazzling him. He hit the brakes hard. The car juddered to a halt, and stalled. The bus roared off, horn blaring. Russell's heart battered against his ribs. Close, a fucking close one. A couple of seconds in it, if that. He killed the radio and drove on at Sunday driver speed.

The wind sliced through the thin strip of trees which had been planted along the roadside as a windbreak. Behind it, he knew there were moors and hills but beyond the trees, the gloved hand of darkness held the landscape in its grip. Where the fuck was he going?

T W E N T Y

A Shallow Depression

Muriel was hacking at the hard ground with a spade and snarling into the frosty night. Her hair was working itself out of the twisted black knot at the back of her head. In the light of a near full moon, her eyes and teeth glinted. Imelda was lumbering about, a soggy stick clamped between her jaws.

—Want a hand?

—I've got two of my own, boy.

—How about a cup of tea?

—Help your damn self.

—I meant I'd make you one.

—What d'you want? Why are you here? I didn't invite you.

—I know. Sorry. I'd have phoned, if you weren't so primitive out here.

—You think I choose to live out here so people can just

jump into their cars and land on me any goddamn time they like?

—Christ, woman, what's eating you?

—Rats, Rusty. One day, maybe I see a teensy field mouse, the next I've got an extended family of rats eating through the floorboards. I shot six already. Don't want to think about how many more there are under there. She resumed hacking at the ground, scraping out a shallow depression.

—I gotta get every goddamned one of them.

—What about poison?

—The dumb dog would eat it.

—Exterminators?

—You know what these guys cost? How come you've got wheels again?

—Courtesy of my ex. As an incentive to go house-hunting.

—Pushy!

Muriel took her spade over to the wall, slid it beneath a small pile of furry carcasses, carried her cargo back to where she had been digging, tipped it into the hole. The dog dropped her drooled-over stick and began sniffing around the rat pit. Muriel shooed her away, poured in half a can of petrol and set a match to it. The flames snapped and leapt from the pit, flames and the throat-catching stench of singed hair. Muriel screwed up her nose and shut her eyes. Her cheeks were streaked with mud.

—Let's go inside, Rusty. I'm okay now.

She folded her arms and frowned into the darkness. She seemed different: more alien, less substantial, as if part of her were absent, wandering through a landscape that Russell couldn't begin to imagine.

They sat on the creaky two-seater couch as far apart as

possible. There was nowhere else to sit. Inside and out, fires crackled.

—Sorry to land on you like this. D'you want me to go?

—It has not been a good day for me, Rusty.

—Me neither. I'm hungry, really hungry. I missed lunch again.

—So? Some people miss lunch every day and still work sixteen-hour shifts. Then again they don't live so long. Do you know what the life expectancy of a rickshaw driver is? Forty, Rusty.

—So if I'd been a rickshaw driver . . .

—You'd be pushing up dandelions by now.

—Daisies, Muriel. Pushing up daisies.

—Dandelions, daisies. You'd be dead, boy. You want to talk about that girlfriend you had?

—Not really. Not at all.

—So, why d'you come out here?

—I don't know. But not to talk about Arlene.

—Good.

Muriel's bedroom wasn't at all like the rest of the cottage. Everywhere else had a functional, if neglected, feel to it, a bit like his own place since Arlene moved out; but the bedroom felt like somewhere . . . internal. Done out in deep reds and purples, the walls were draped with embroidered cloths depicting mythical birds and beasts, and heavy velvet curtains were drawn against the still crackling rat pyre. Behind the bed, beads and small bones hung in loops beneath gilt-framed photographs of neat, smiling groups of Filipinos. There were no solo portraits.

—We don't think being alone is a virtue, Rusty.

For such a small person, Muriel had a great deal of strength. In her fingertips at least, which were kneading his back like pizza dough. Arlene had never been one for massage. Not even at the beginning in what might have passed as the romantic phase of their relationship. Couldn't be bothered; too much palaver, too time-consuming – no, massage had never been on Arlene's menu.

Muriel's fingers were searching for his non-existent waistline.

—Couldn't you concentrate on the better bits?

—Which bits did you have in mind?

—Look, why are you doing this, Muriel?

—Because it's good for you, dummy. Relaxed body, relaxed mind . . .

—I'm not really your type, am I?

—What's my type, Rusty? You got some information I don't have?

—I mean, I'm not exactly God's gift.

—I never met a man who was God's gift. Met one to two who were God's mistake, though. But what's your problem? You're here. You're happy, no? You rather be with your old girlfriend?

—No way, Muriel, no way.

—Good. Okay, now let's see how those better bits are doing. Muriel slapped his arse briskly. Don't want to get too relaxed, Rusty. Roll over.

Russell was content to do as he was told. As he rolled on to his back, his cock swung up, quivered and strained towards the ceiling.

—Okay! said Muriel. So the forecast is good, is it?

She slid down the bed. She was still wearing one of her ragged, all-encompassing jerseys. He felt overexposed.

—Don't you want to take that thing off?

—Later.

She knelt astride his knees, grinning wickedly, and

lowered her head, her mouth closing around his cock and her tongue beginning to work on it with the same deft agility that her fingertips had dealt with his shoulderblades. All physical sensation became concentrated in one urgently throbbing organ.

—Eh, listen, em . . . shouldn't we . . . shouldn't I put something on?

It was incredible really that he was able to remember the practicalities. As Muriel's throat opened wider, he tried to concentrate on something else, anything else, anything to take the edge off the sensation of her tongue coiling, lips squeezing and sliding, squeezing and sliding . . .

Without warning, she released her grip and withdrew.

—Relax, Rusty. It's taken care of.

—How did you do that?

Muriel grinned again and pulled her jersey over her head.

It was all so easy, so smooth, one touch leading to another and another, no knocking of knees, no squashed arms or grating bones, no impatience, no rush, just the sound of synchronised breathing, the way it was meant to be but hardly ever was . . .

—Okay, now?

—Fine. Fine.

—I'll put off the light, now.

His body was still and heavy as death but his brain was engaged in relentless eruptions of random activity. He was not thinking. He needed to do some thinking, some quick thinking as soon as possible, but nothing bearing any resemblance to a thought was formulating. His body was telling his brain that it was too knackered for anything at all but his brain wasn't admitting defeat; it was on overdrive, recycling rubbish. No, really he didn't want any more thoughts at all, he was deluding himself about thoughts. A solution was what he needed but all that appeared on Russell's interior screen were malignant clusters of trouble, multiplying.

The room was very dark. From the gap beneath the door, a thin scar of firelight throbbed but otherwise there was nothing but a dense, palpable blackness. Muriel, curled up against his back, was snoring softly. He could hear a faint scrabbling: embers breaking up and crumbling into ash, a rat which had escaped Muriel's gun and death by fire, an internal disturbance? The room had shrunk to the space between his ears. If it wasn't in his ears, it must be out there, the scrabbling. If it didn't stop there was no way he was going to get to sleep, though sleep was the only sensible option. His brain should take the hint, do itself a favour and shut down. It wasn't the fire. The scrabbling was too close. If it wasn't in his ears, it must be in the room. He lay motionless, barely breathing until he realised what he was hearing: Imelda pawing the floorboards, chasing rabbits — or rats — in her sleep.

It was the middle of the night and he was out in the sticks, in a rat-infested cottage with Muriel — again, wide awake. He got out of bed quietly and felt for the door. In the living room the fire had subsided to a flickering red glow. Above the mantelpiece Muriel's gun seemed to be moving. At first he thought it was just a trick of the light but no, the gun, suspended by a leather strap, was definitely swinging gently. Hot air currents from the fire must be responsible. There was always an explanation for something like that, if you looked far enough. Unlike human behaviour. Human behaviour was a mystery to him, an impenetrable, irritating mystery.

He draped Muriel's dressing gown over his shoulders, poured himself a whisky and mooched around. In the window alcove he noticed another framed photograph. With only the dying firelight, it wasn't easy to see clearly but he could tell it was a class photo of some kind: three rows of young Filipinas in white blouses and dark skirts smiling obediently for the camera. Muriel was in the front row – there was no mistaking her grin. The photo was faded and appeared to be damaged by mildew; there were black spots all over it. But it wasn't mildew; the spots had been carefully inked in to blot out many of the smiling faces.

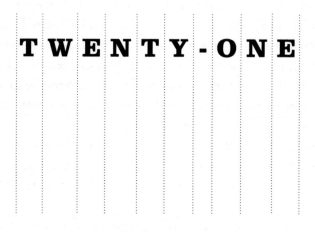

TWENTY-ONE

Where Are They Now?

Russell woke to the sound of Muriel's van clattering down the track. Why did the woman have to rush off right now? It was the weekend; the two of them could have had a nice snuggly lie in together. Maybe she'd just nipped down to the village for a newspaper or a pint of milk. He shut his eyes again, breathed in the warm, salty smell of the sheets and would have drifted back to sleep had Imelda not attempted to burrow in beside him.

—Gerroff.

Snuffling head shake. Low, deep-throated growl.

—You heard me. You know what I'm saying. Off. Down.

The dog was nothing if not determined, curling into a compacted mass of hair and teeth and the only thing for it was to shove both hands under her belly and roll her, like a hairy log, on to the floor. After such an ignominious landing, Imelda got the message and slunk off to the living room.

As Muriel didn't return with or without breakfast, he made himself a slice of toast and a cup of instant coffee. Imelda began to paw his feet and whimper every time he swallowed until he found the dog food and dumped some rabbit chunks in jelly on to a dish. The dog gulped it down in a matter of seconds and didn't show any obvious signs of gratitude. Still, it gave up whimpering and left his feet alone.

Russell sat at the table by the window and looked out on what to be honest was a dismal view: some small fields and a clump of scraggy woodland had been squeezed into insignificance by the legacy of dead industry; slag heap after slag heap, rust-coloured pyramids, pyres to industry's dead tyrants – iron, steel, coal. A used-up, burnt-out landscape, a desolation of abandoned quarries, crumbling factories and warehouses, a wasteland where the ground had been ravaged and left to rot. Even the microchip industry which had emerged from the ashes of quarrying was already on the way out. Somebody somewhere else could and would do it cheaper.

The first time he'd stayed over, Muriel had made bacon and eggs and great coffee but had touched nothing herself.

—Once a week I fast, Rusty. To feel the fire. To remember.

What fire? What burning memories was the woman harbouring? Did he really want to know? He straightened up the bedroom and cleaned out the grate. As a boy, he'd been mesmerised by the whole process of laying a fire: the empty, dull grey grate, the twists of newspaper about to consign murderers, politicians and film stars to the flames, the lattice of sticks, last night's cinders, the coal itself, black and shiny as the jet beads old ladies wore for funerals. As a boy, lighting the fire was the only household chore he'd volunteered for, putting a match to the twists of paper, waiting for the cold neutral tones to burst into hot reds, yellows, blues, greens.

It was cold in the cottage without the fire. Muriel didn't seem to have any other kind of heating. He hung around for a bit, expecting to hear the van at any moment but the quiet was only disturbed by nattering crows. The pale sky glittered behind bare, frosted trees. Using their beaks as pickaxes, the crows attacked the hard ground. The dog, which had been following him around since he got out of bed, threw herself at the door and barked loudly. When he let her out, she lolloped off to the coal box and stopped in front of it, snuffling and quivering.

In Russell's experience, something other than coal was often to be found in a coal box. As a boy, he'd harboured hopes of discovering a fluffy rabbit or wounded pigeon but time and again when he'd been sent out in the dark to fill up the scuttle, it had been rats he'd disturbed. And a stoat, once, tunnelling through dross and slinking beneath the drop hatch. God, the ability of small, furry animals to render themselves boneless . . .

—Is it a rat, Imelda? Do you smell a rat?

Imelda was too worked up by the scent to respond. He'd as soon have ignored it but you didn't need a degree in biochemistry to know that there was a population explosion on Muriel's doorstep.

He hadn't handled a gun since he was a teenager, when he and his pal Sandy – whose dad was a farmer – had lined up tin cans and cast themselves as flint-eyed sharp-shooters – Eastwood style – though they knew fine that they lacked the requisite bone structure, tan and charisma.

He fetched the gun and a couple of cartridges from the row on the mantelpiece – Muriel was not short of ammunition. Imelda seemed to know the score: as Russell slid two cartridges into the chamber and kicked open the lid of the coal box, she backed off and sat down on the doorstep, panting expectantly. At first, all he could see was a silvery blackness; then a bristling snout pushed up through the coal, and another and another. Twitching whiskers and gleaming teeth. Russell stepped back, took aim hastily and fired into the coal box. A cloud of soot puffed up in his face, the wooden walls of the coal box collapsed and two, three, four adult rats made their scrabbling exodus. They were fast, hell of a fast for the big bastards that they were. Russell wiped the soot from his eyes and fired again at the path, hitting nothing but an old window Muriel had rigged up as a frame for seedlings. It smashed noisily, spraying shards of glass all over the path. The rats vanished, unscathed. Imelda padded over, sat down at his feet and rolled reproachful eyes at him.

—See what you've made me do? Now stay.

Gloomily contrite, the dog stayed, tail thumping the ground. Russell went back inside and hung the shotgun on its hook. Just as well Muriel hadn't been around to witness his attempts at rat-catching; she'd have been less than impressed. But what did that matter? He'd never intended to impress Muriel, never intended to have anything at all to do with the woman and here he was getting tangled up in her domestic problems. His own home was being stripped away from him: what was he doing about that?

A brush and shovel. The kitchen cupboard was a shambles of tools and assorted junk piled in on top of each other. He could see a brush, wedged in at the back, behind a battered zinc wash bucket, a drill and a stack of old newspapers tied in bundles with garden twine. When he tried to extricate it, a bundle of papers fell off the stack, burst open and slithered down into a heap at his feet. An assortment of British dailies and an English language paper based in Manila, the papers dated back about ten years. Why would Muriel hang on to this mouldy old stuff? As he gathered them up, a front-page photograph caught his eye: a group photograph of smiling young women. The newsprint was yellowed and dusty.

Class of '88, the paper said, ***Where are they now?***

Science students with a bright future ahead of them, these young women met together out of school to talk about things other than grades and boyfriends. At first they were careful what they said and where they said it but in Manila a safe place to talk and safe words to speak are not so easy to find. Sometimes, too, they were so angry that they forgot to be careful. They knew there were many people like them who wanted rid of the president but of course, he knew that too and he would do anything to stay in power. He had already called a snap election, to wrongfoot the opposition. All they wanted was a fair vote and a result which reflected the choice of the people.

The first death was made to look like a traffic accident, a very bad traffic accident, but these things happen every day. The girls were shaken and saddened by the loss of a friend, but not immediately suspicious. The second fatality, death by a thousand cuts, immediately after a meeting, was clearly no accident but a brutal warning. There was no doubt by then that the students had been dangerously indiscreet. The dead girl's parents were too frightened to make a formal report to the police and begged the girl's friends to stick to their studies and mourn their daughter only in their hearts.

Some stayed away from their studies, others attended classes

in silence, kept their eyes to the ground, lived like sleepwalkers or
slow ghosts. But these young people could only live like the dead
for so long before hope began to blossom. New pockets of
support were reported; all over the country people were risking
their skins for the chance of a better life. You can smell hope, like
a sweet breeze rippling through the toxic air of the city and,
slowly, fear ebbs and rage ignites the blood. Meetings resume
and so does trouble; beatings, shootings, beheadings. After the
beheadings, those still alive went into hiding. It was that or wait
for the death squads. They are hiding still.

With a cold blast of realisation, Russell took the newspaper through to the living room and compared the photo to the one on the wall with the blacked-out faces; they were, as he'd expected, identical. He sat down at the table and stared at the newspaper until the print began to blur and jump. The woman he'd spent the night with had a past he couldn't even begin to imagine. The stuff she must carry around with her, the memories, how did she keep going, how did she sleep at night, go into work in the morning, how did she keep smiling, for God's sake?

Still hoping that Muriel would return at any moment and not relishing the thought of being caught rifling through her stuff, he tied up the papers and shoved them back in the cupboard. Outside, he swept the broken glass into a pile and covered the remains of the coal shed with a piece of plastic sheeting. He did the dishes from the night before and gave the dog a drink. He thought about leaving a note but didn't know what he wanted to say. He waited around a bit longer, then gave up. The dog scritched at the living room window as he drove off.

Ribbons of torn plastic snagged on barbed wire. Sheep grazed inside the charred shell of a farmhouse. Drystane dykes were returning to the piles of rock they'd been built from. All the way down the track he expected, hoped to see the pink van bumping towards him but passed nothing except a couple of scraggy chickens which had strayed from the farm at the end of the road. He crawled through the village: no van, no Muriel. It was a low, drab, two-shop village. One displayed ancient knitting patterns and hostess sets – whatever they were – in wrinkled cellophane wrappers. Muscling in on the faded and outmoded, the new convenience store had plastered its windows with dayglo fliers proclaiming bumper savings on the current essentials of life: nappies, monster tins of baked beans, booze, confidential loan advice. Most of the locals out doing their shopping looked poor, cold and old.

He'd forgotten the sharp bend at the slip road and had to brake. The *Property Guide* slithered off the passenger seat. A small bottle slid the width of the dashboard before it, too, hit the floor. Within seconds Arlene's perfume – a tart mixture of seaweed and citrus – had invaded and conquered the air he was breathing. Stuck behind a tractor, he had time to look around. Even the seasons were behind the city: flimsy golden leaves still glinted like coins on a chain of gangly poplars lining the road. Ribbed brown sleeves of earth stretched towards the slag heaps. Crows on the wires, sheep munching turnips, a dark parabola of geese flapping south. Russell picked up the *Property Guide* and stuffed it into the glove compartment, along with Arlene's now empty perfume bottle. He rolled down the window. An icy blast whirled round the car but instead of dispersing the scent, the draught pushed it deeper into his nostrils. He shut the window and drove back to town with the fan full on, allowing the fart smell of turnips to overpower Arlene's perfume which had a slap in the face quality he didn't care for at all.

Mrs Ramasawmy was sitting at the till of Nice Price, on her packing crate, staring at the flickering grey screen of the recently installed security system. Her husband Panjit was slowly unloading a crate of milk into the bottom shelf of the fridge. Parveen and Sonia stood beside their mother, silently watching the door. There was no one else in the shop. Russell swung round the aisle, grabbing some bits and pieces.

—Want a bag? said Mrs Ramasawmy, without taking her eyes from the screen.

—Please. Hello there, girls. Too cold to play out?

Sonia turned to him, her eyes huge and dark. She looked older, somehow, grownup. Parveen's face was streaked with the snail-tracks of dried tears.

—We don't play today, said Sonia flatly. We stay in the shop, with our mother and father.

—We are mourning, said Parveen. We are very sad.

—You don't need to tell everybody.

—I'm not telling everybody. I'm just telling this one person.

Panjit had the top half of his body inside the fridge. Twisting awkwardly, he glanced through the glass door and his own squint spectacles at his assembled family then wearily continued to stock the fridge. Mrs Ramasawmy began to pack Russell's purchases into a plastic bag which was barely strong enough to hold the milk never mind the whisky.

—My sister's baby dead, she said. In Delhi. First baby. Plague.

Russell's eyes flitted uncomfortably from mother to

daughters, to Panjit crouched at the fridge, to the screen which showed his own face looking up at it, to the counter where his messages lay, lumpy and inert.

—God, I'm sorry, really. That's terrible.

It wasn't enough. He wanted to say something more but what? What was there to say? There were never enough words for tragedy. Or the right ones.

—My sister's husband queued all night outside the hospital, waiting for medicine. There was medicine, but not enough. Every time somebody came to the door he called out: *Please, my baby is sick*. But the door was open and shut, open and shut. Too many people. Too many sick people. Today we are very sad.

Parveen began to cry. Sonia glared at her sister: the older girl's lip quivered but her eyes were steady, stoic.

—Terrible, said Mrs Ramasawmy. Terrible. Five pounds fifty-seven, dear.

Russell picked up his groceries and shut the door behind him as gently as possible.

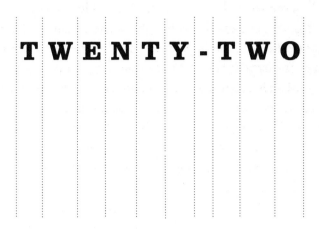

TWENTY-TWO

Patriots

It really needed doing up, the bathroom. The wallpaper frilled up from the skirting board like a new kind of fungus and around the sink it was dotted with toothpaste splatters. As for the bath, it was probably a health hazard. But the shower worked and he felt cold, grubby, contaminated. He turned up the thermostat and shut his eyes. India; what did he know about India except what he'd seen in travel brochures and documentaries? Skeletal men in snow-white loincloths, rickshaws, saris, sitars, elephants, kids in carpet factories shackled to their looms, kids banged up in brothels, kids scavenging from rubbish tips. The crowds, yes he could picture the queues and crowds, the clamouring needy throng outside the high barred doors of a hospital, its patience pushed past the limit. Demand dwarfing supply. That was the way of it, a constant race to keep pace with the microbes of the world. A race that could never be won. As one disease faded into obscurity, another would hatch out and grab the limelight. The Pest Maiden's appetite was insatiable.

Russell washed himself thoroughly. He'd always found washing to be beneficial though even that small pleasure had been diminished by reading Fox's exaggerated descriptions of his ablutions. So he liked a good scrub and occasionally splashed out on body care products, quality shaving gear in particular; there was nothing weird about that, nothing kinky or even eccentric. His work demanded that he was not only fastidious about personal hygiene but also clean shaven at all times. As human hair and skin were the main carriers of germs, beards were banned from most departments. Besides, Arlene claimed that men hid their flaws behind facial hair and as far as he was concerned, he had nothing to hide. The body was a machine after all, prone to attack from inside and out. If you didn't do some regular maintenance work, it began to break down. But Fox had depicted him – in the persona of Leslie Little – as verging on the obsessive; showering three times a day, scrubbing himself red raw with some kind of masochistic Japanese exfoliator and having deviant fantasies while he was at it. Crap. As he scrubbed himself with a matted chunk of loofah, scrubbed until his skin tingled, as the hot water streamed down his back, he had a perfectly natural, murderous fantasy.

The phone rang. And rang. He turned off the water, slung a towel over his shoulders and dripped through the icy hall. Now completely stripped of wallpaper, it had the harbour-at-low-tide odour of old paste and damp plaster.

—Are you busy?

—Depends. What d'you want, Arlene?

He should have stayed in the shower.

—A word.

—I've had enough words from you to last me a lifetime.

—Have you been using the car?

—Not for house-hunting.

—I didn't call about the flat.

—What else could you possibly want to talk to me about?

—You know. You know fine.

—Know what?

—You're a useless liar.

—I haven't had a great deal of practice at lying. Unlike some.

—Don't go.

—Go? Go where?

—Christ, Russell, don't make me spell it out.

On the other end of the line, Russell could hear a radio crackling in the background, the familiar din of Boon's kitchen and Arlene snatching a shallow, impatient drag on a cigarette.

—You know Frankie's coming to town.

—*Frankie*, is it? I did hear something about *Frankie*. On the radio. In fact, I heard the man himself. But I wasn't really paying attention.

—I know you better than you think, Russell.

—And I know you, Arlene, better than I want to.

—You don't know me at all. If you'd known me a bit better in the first place . . .

—So it was my fault you fell into bed with *Frankie*?

—It wasn't anybody's fault. It just happened. Once, Russell, one night. A year ago. And we haven't been in touch since. Still fucking the Filipina?

—Her name's Muriel. How do you know about her?

—News travels fast, Russell.

—Muriel's *a friend*.

—You don't have women friends, Russell.

—Maybe I've changed. What d'you want, anyway?

—Forget it.

—What d'you mean, forget it? You got me out of the fucking shower. You might as well say what you were going to say now that I'm freezing my arse off in this half-decorated hallway . . .

Arlene hung up. Russell didn't consider calling her back.

He was swithering between a fry-up and a take-away kebab, curry or pizza when, from across the street, he heard a door being slammed. It was followed by yells, running feet, several dull thuds, a long low groan. He stayed in the kitchen, hoping the scuffle would burn itself out quickly but the sounds of bodies colliding continued. It was early for a fight. They were popular in the small hours, after the latest pubs had shut their doors, the ideal time to cause maximum disturbance to the neighbourhood. It was early for a fight and too close for comfort. He went through to the front room and squinted through a chink in the curtain, trying to see what was happening outside without drawing attention to himself.

Three against one; three pairs of boots laying into a body curled up on the pavement, clutching a broad-headed brush. A wallpaper brush. Lag. Lag beneath the boots of the patriots from across the road. The patriots and a pal, a fucking girl. Russell marched to the door, flung it open and froze. Three of them. What the fuck could he do against three of them? He should have called the police: that would have been the sensible thing to do, that was what they were paid for, but he hadn't thought quickly enough and now the action had been cut and all eyes were on him.

The girl, like a sleekit pet, snarled at him.

—Got a fuckin problem?

She ran her tongue over the steel fishhook which speared her bottom lip.

—You lot will have a problem, if you don't bugger off. The police are on their way.

—Like fuck, they fuckin are.

Lag groaned.

—Shut it, you.

The girl jabbed the toe of her boot against Lag's ear.

—Christsakes, lay off him.

—Gonnae make me? Gonnae make me, ya wee shite?

No thought was involved, no decision. A chemical reaction, an internal explosion propelled Russell to charge into their midst, grab hold of Lag, hoist him to his feet, drag him through the gate and push him up the short path. Only after he'd shut and bolted the door did Russell feel pain from the kicks he'd received. And realise the risk he'd taken.

—Wee shite! D'ye no ken, the only heroes are deid heroes!

Lag sank to the floor, groaning quietly as the patriots flung something at the door, then rampaged down the street, their shouts battering between the tenement walls. God help wherever they were heading.

Russell looked down at Lag and instantly wished he hadn't. Blood was seeping from an eye, an ear, from the hand still loyally clutching the fucking wallpaper brush. The kid tried to speak; blood bubbled from his mouth.

—aaaaahhhhmmmmmmgonnnnnnab eeeeeeeeee fine.

—'Course you are, man, 'course . . . Russell mumbled as the floor rushed up to meet him.

TWENTY-THREE

Blood The Memorious

Blood the river — wider deeper faster, infinitely more treacherous than the mind's uncatalogued emporium of spent events. Blood the vessel, blood the channel. Blood the ebb, the flow, the roaring chorus of kinship, the circular song. The surge downstream. Spring, torrent, flood. Effluence, effluvium. Blood's games: Chinese whispers, pass the parcel, catch-kiss. Dispenser of rewards, consolations, booby prizes; hook-nose, cleft chin, hen toes, knock-knees, jug ears, a frown from the mother's side, a frown from the father's. An insensitive stomach, a fragile heart, colourblindness, perfect pitch, dodgy synapses. Blood the travel bag. Blood the passport. Blood the ticket, plane, the boat, train, coach, cart, the mule, the camel. Blood the hold, the trunk, backpack, suitcase. Blood the money-belt, credit card. Always the journey, never the destination. Blood the midge, the rat, the leech, the lamprey. Blood the graze, scratch, sore, lesion, the laceration, the open wound, the scab, scar. Blood the bottle, flask, chalice, phial. Blood the host to inbred loyalties, cataclysmic affiliations, molotov cocktails, fatal liaisons. Blood the hunter-gatherer, looter and pillager, dealer in the begged and borrowed, the renovated, rehashed, regenerated. Home-maker / home-breaker. Blood the roller-coaster, global grid, the labyrinth, the catacombs, subway, sewer . . .

—Are you sure you're all right now, Mr Fairley?

—Fine. I'm fine.

—Just as well that poor lad had enough of his wits about him to call an ambulance, eh?

—You can say that again. How is he?

—Sleeping. Best thing for him at the moment.

Russell tossed his empty plastic teacup into the bin and hurried towards the A & E exit, and merciful darkness.

**You've got it in you to save a life
We've had your sweat and tears, now we want your blood
125 gallons a day and still going down
Without you, we can't operate
This Christmas, it's better to give than to receive.**

The last was illustrated with little santas hefting blood bags. The Transfusion Service tried its best but even in its appeals for donors, it was beginning to sound like a limited company. Which it was probably on the way to becoming.

Russell's symptoms: lightheadedness, dislocation, embarrassment (acute), humiliation (chronic), shame, self-loathing, a pressing need to be away from the brisk, contemptuous gaze of the staff nurse.

TWENTY-FOUR

A Rolex

The wind snapped at the ankles, slapped the face, snatched up the priest's hurried words and scattered them like litter across the bowed heads of the mourners. Grit skittered along the gravel pathway. Overhead, gulls screamed and clouds raced away. The white ash box which held the night-watchman's body was lowered creakily into the ground. Of the tight huddle on the far side of the grave, Russell recognised a few folk from the plant – the delivery boys, Jake and Davey, Myra and Sadie from the downstream processing and two or three others whose faces were familiar from the cafeteria. Jake and Davey stood stiffly, hands clasped and feet apart, eyes fixed on their feet. Myra and Sadie, both big sturdy women, linked grey-coated arms. By isolating themselves from the official works envoy of Everett, Morris and Russell, the workers were demonstrating their allegiance to the friends and family camp. Russell, too, would have been happier on their side than his own.

Bobby's resting place was a blasted, muddy hump in the middle of a crumbling post-war housing scheme. It was a modest cemetery, the headstones uniformly small and plain. No tall, consoling evergreens lined the paths, no pensive stone angels kept watch over souls though most of the plots were well-tended, with trimmed shrubs and frosty bunches of flowers in plastic vases. The red brick of the wall surrounding the burial ground was camouflaged by layers of graffiti. Beyond the immediate, bleak vicinity, stood the crags, hunched and imposing, a dark congregation. Further south, under a leaden sky, the coastline, like mercury, curled in a blinding silver slick. The windows of the Power Station caught the setting winter sun on their panes and blazed like a furnace.

With a dull clunk, the coffin hit the bottom of the grave. A small woman in a scarlet duffel coat and purple trousers bent down, picked up a handful of earth, threw it in. The mourners turned away. As he led the way to the car park, the priest pressed a bible to his head, to stop his wispy silver hair from blowing into his eyes.

The smell of last night's sweet and sour prawns still hung around the red, gold and black dining room of the Lucky Kumquat Family Hotel. Flock wallpaper and thick carpeting absorbed the already muted conversation. Circular tables had been laid with cups and saucers and plates of sandwiches. Two young women in striped waistcoats and plain black skirts had begun to dispense tea and coffee from large pots. The bar, which ran along the back wall of the room, was open for business.

—We won't stay long, said Everett. We're just here to put in an appearance.

Everett flipped his teaspoon against his not-yet-filled cup. In spite of the fact that they were on the far side of the room with several tables before them expecting service, Morris was waving hopefully at the waitresses. Like the other already-full tables, theirs had been set for eight but it looked as though the three of them would be stuck with each other for the duration. The other plant workers had seated themselves as far away as possible.

—If you ask me, Morrison, said Everett, I can't see why anybody wants to be buried in this day and age. In the past, superstition or religious belief might have stood in the way of cremation but nowadays . . .

—True, said Morris. But there was also a practical reason why people shunned the furnace. It was common knowledge that – by accident more often than design – people were, on occasion, buried while they were still alive. You might even say that those who insisted on burial were looking on the bright side, by entertaining the possibility of, as it were, coming back from the dead.

—Cremation's more practical, Everett insisted. What with the price of a plot – and that's something that'll never go down – not in this city. And then you've got the labour costs; I mean, for the deceased or for those left behind, where's the benefit in burial?

Russell felt like a traitor. When the news had got out about Bobby's death, the feeling on the factory floor was that more could have been done for the man, more would have been done for him, if somebody had kicked up a fuss on his behalf. He'd made what had appeared to be a good recovery, he was sent home from hospital, contracted pneumonia and died a few days later. This was not the plant's fault, or the hospital's, this was bad timing, bad luck, bad habits: life as Bobby'd known it. A life which had aged him prematurely. Russell had put Bobby down as mid-fifties but the man had only been forty-four. Forty-four! Just three years older than him!

At the bar, Russell ordered a whisky and stood drinking it with his back firmly set against the room. He became aware of a woman at his elbow, the same woman who'd thrown earth on Bobby's coffin at it had descended to its regulation depth. Her steely hair was pinned back with clasps and her pinched face held a tense, rigid smile.

—A bad day for burying and no mistake. Mr Fairley? Ah'm Dora, Bobby's sister. Father McDiarmid might as well have been speaking Yiddish for all ah could make oot but we cannae choose the weather when our time comes for makin the transition frae this world tae the next. If you ask me, Bobby's well oot o this yin. Anyway, he's got nae wife or bairns so ah thought he'd mibbe like *you* . . . tae hae this. Dora dug into her handbag, pulled out a chunky metal watch and plonked it on the slippery, wood-effect bar top.

—It's a Rolex.

—No no, look thanks but . . . something like that should surely go to a relative.

—Pricey, they are, but it's okay, Bobby didnae pay for it. Found it on the beach at Skegness. Lucky that way, he wis, aye findin stuff. Nane o us'll use it. Wear yin o them roond oor bit and some bampot's gonnae take it intae his heid that ye're worth burglin. A good timekeeper, so it is.

—Like Bobby. Bobby was a good timekeeper.

—Wis he now? That's a surprise. Aye a last minute Lizzie when he wis a bairn. Right, well, ah'd better get back tae ma table or ah'll get masel a bad reputation.

With that, Dora scurried away from her dead brother's Rolex. While he finished his drink, Russell stared stupidly at the watch. As he couldn't think of anything better to do with it, he slipped it into his pocket.

Everett's BMW purred down the treeless drive, crouched at the junction then leapt into the road and began purring again. Russell had taken the back seat, hoping that Morris and Everett wouldn't bother to make the extra effort to speak to him.

—Well, that seemed to go as well as could be expected. Don't you think, Fairley?

—Suppose so.

—Was that a relative of Mr Doyle's you were speaking to at the bar, Fairley?

—Uh huh.

—The dress code for funerals seems to have gone out the window nowadays.

—Mmmm.

—Odd place to have the reception, a Chinese restaurant.

—The sandwiches weren't up to much.

—And we've missed lunch.

—So we have.

Mid-afternoon, the sky dark enough to merit side lights. The traffic was dense and sluggish. School was out. Kids streamed out of the gates and spilled on to the pavement, puffing on fags and spewing out curses. How many of them would, in the not-too distant future, find themselves taking the road for Plasma Glen?

At the turn-off, visibility was further reduced by the high stone walls and the scrawl of treetops above them. Russell knew the bends only too well, knew what was round the next sharp left. In the deepening gloom, the plant rose up ahead, solid and black. Birds had gathered on the overhead cables, waiting to claim whatever the 'dozers turned up as they prepared the ground for the construction of yet another new, improved unit, another attempt to combat the eternally ingenious onslaught of microbes. In the meantime, bacteria liberated from the disturbed soil would be swarming around the filters for the air-conditioning system, trying to find a way in.

Russell's symptoms: mutinous blood

TWENTY-FIVE

Drinking Air

—So, Mr Fox, where exactly did you find your inspiration for your latest opus? Did you dredge it from your putrid imagination or did you have to indulge in some hands-on research? You see, Mr Fox, some parts of the story you wrote seemed to me hell of a familiar, so bloody familiar that . . . no, no, showing your hand too soon . . .

The doorbell. The doorbell again.

—Hi, Rusty. Can I come in?

Muriel's hair was pinned back in a glossy croissant and small, silver leaves dangled from her ears. Otherwise she was as usual; bulked out by layers of rough, dog-smelling wool. Imelda didn't seem keen on visiting. Once Muriel had dragged her through the door, the dog flopped on to the hall rug and embarked on a litany of tetchy barks and doom-ridden howls. Muriel hugged Imelda then yelled at her but neither strategy had much effect on the racket.

—Can you leave the dog in the hall?

Russell had the kind of headache which made him feel he was being punished for something, a Calvinist, guilt-laden headache.

—Shut my poor baby out in this icebox? Let my poppet shiver and shake and catch a chill? You gonna pay the vet bill?

—It's not *that* cold.

—Sure as hell is, Rusty. Freezing. You got central heating, you don't use it. Me, I'd have it on all the time. Got a blanket?

—This really has to be a short visit. I'm on my way out.

—Gee thanks. Is this what you call hospitality? In my country . . . huh, who cares about my country but paedophiles on holiday?

The only place to sit was the bedroom; the kitchen was a health hazard, the livingroom was still under dust sheets and Lag wouldn't be wielding a wallpaper brush for some time. The kid was 'settled', communicating minimally and, for now, requesting no visitors. *Not surprising when your face looks like a chopping board*, the ward sister had added with professional detachment.

—Usually I feel strong, said Muriel. Good about being in touch with those other times. But tonight, no, tonight is not good. I have this flapping inside, like bats.

—You're hungry, woman. You need to eat.

—I know I'm bloody hungry, Rusty, but this is something else.

Muriel flung herself on to the rumpled bed and looked around. There was nothing much to look at. In addition to the botanical drawings from the living room, Arlene had also removed her screen prints of vegetables from the bedroom walls. He'd never paid much attention to them when they were there but their absence was depressing. On the mushroom-grey walls, paler squares marked where the magnified representations of garlic, aubergine, fennel and capsicum had hung.

Russell's clothes were all over the place. Clean clothes at least: he'd been trying on shirts, jeans, even ties, though he'd quickly scrapped the idea of a tie. He had to be himself tonight, an improved but still recognisable *version* of himself, without looking as if he'd made a special effort. That had taken a hell of a lot longer to achieve than he'd meant it to.

—So this is where you sleep?

—You're seeing it.

—It feels lonely in here, Rusty.

—Yeah, well . . . I have to go out soon.

—You told me already.

—I'm having a quick drink. D'you want anything?

—Bring me an empty glass. I'll pretend.

—You're nuts.

—Everybody's nuts.

In the kitchen, Russell poured himself a whisky and – against his better judgement – found a clean glass for Muriel's make-believe. He, too, was aware of an internal disturbance, a churning in the guts, the cause of which had nothing to do with hunger.

He should have thought; he should have remembered: it would only have taken a moment to slip the bloody thing under the pillow . . .

—This looks like racy bedtime reading, Rusty. But why all the underlining? You doing an OU degree in dirty books?

—Forget it, just forget it.

But he hadn't forgotten it. In spite of so much else vying

for priority status, nothing had so far diverted him from his purpose, his desire, his obsession for vengeance. Under no circumstances was Fox going to skulk away unscathed.

Already the new jacket needed a brush. It was no longer the deep, reassuring navy it had been in the shop; dust had settled on the shoulders and some unidentifiable crud from his pints with homeless Peter had found its way on to the lapels. There used to be a clothes brush but he hadn't been able to find it; another household item which must have found a new home in Boon's basement bistro. Absences were what was left of his life with Arlene: things missing.

Russell gave the jacket a stiff-palmed slap and put it on. He flexed his elbows and rotated his shoulders, did up the buttons, undid them. Nice and easy; no restriction of movement. A well-fitting garment, for a change.

—What d'you think? he said.

—I think that guy got something wrong.

—I mean the jacket. It's new.

—Very nice . . . but this passionfruit stuff. He's making out that eating passionfruit equals hot sex, right? Like because it's got all those seeds and pulp and if you squeeze the skin the insides squirt out like you know what?

—If you say so.

—That's what the cover's saying. But the passion relates to the *flower*, not the fruit. Christ's passion: the stigmata represent the nails, the stamens His wounds, the fringed corona the crown of thorns. Aphrodisiac, bullshit. We give kids the fruit juice to help them sleep.

Russell slugged at his whisky. Muriel sipped on some whisky-flavoured air. On the other side of the hall door, Imelda howled and scrabbled.

—She likes you, Rusty.

—I thought you said she liked all men.

—But she really likes you.

If the dog liked him at all, it was because of his smell; nothing more to it than pheromones. Was it the same with people? Was attraction all just a question of smell? If you believed the ads, a change of scent could transform any mediocre specimen into a scent-of-the-season Adonis. All that was needed was a quick splash of ethyl alcohol laced with extracts from a sperm whale's scrotum. Or secretion of cat. Ambergris, civet. But if so, why didn't it go on working? Why did the signals cease to have the desired effect? Before they went out, Russell wrote *Carwash* on the memory board beside the door.

They had to leave Imelda on the street, tied to a lamppost.

—What if somebody steals her? said Muriel. You know what people do to dogs?

—You don't have to come in. I don't want you to come in. I could meet you later.

—Uh uh.

Muriel ripped open a packet of chocolate drops and set it down in front of Imelda.

—Okay, babylove, don't eat these all at once. And if anybody lays a finger on you, bark like shit, okay?

Imelda snuffled and made a start on her canine candy.

As all the seats had been taken, they had to stand at the back. A woman in a gecko-green blouse was tapping a finger in the air, counting heads. Was this the same woman who had hosted Fox's previous *Meet the Author* session? If so, Fox's details were accurate: *A brisk woman with a bossy voice, skirt straining over a dumpling of a belly* . . . How did she feel about her bit part in *Passionfruit*? Was she too burning up with unrequited vengeance or thrilled to get a mention?

When Green Blouse had finished her head count,

frowned at the freeloaders hanging around the drinks table and shamed them into joining the body of the audience, she disappeared through a door marked *Staff Only*. Was that where Fox was holed up? And Arlene, was she lurking back there with him, the pair of them catching up on lost time before he shot his load about their intimate ins and outs to a roomful of strangers? Russell had checked out the audience – squeezed between Eastern Religions and Personal Growth – three times already. No sign of Arlene. At the wine table, a couple of neat young staff in monogrammed T-shirts were herding unused glasses into a gleaming, serried flock. In the body of the shop, solitary browsers inched intently from shelf to shelf. At the door, a cash register bleeped out bar codes. Muriel grinned out of the window and waved to the dog.

Russell swallowed a mouthful of purplish wine. It tasted bitter, stung his tongue and blistered his lips. His throat, too, felt raw, scalded. Christ, the roving streptococci were busy targeting the very part of him which he needed to be in working order.

—Ladies and gentlemen, I'd like to welcome this month's guest, all the way from *The Big Apple* . . .

He could have understood Arlene being tempted by plenty of other men – younger, better-looking, in better shape, with better jobs, dress-sense, with more money, taste, personality and so on – but what did this guy have going for him that he didn't? While Green Blouse was doing her introduction – and mangling most of Fox's titles in the process – the author's gaze batted between the ceiling and his tan loafers, his left hand worried the back of his neck and the right appeared to have found something interesting at the very bottom of his trouser pocket.

After the polite, welcoming applause had died down, Green Blouse retreated and Fox was left on his own; he looked terrified. One hand clung to the table, the other worried the back of his pale, thinning head.

—Hi, he said. It's great to be back here. I have very fond memories of your city.

In a thin, damp voice he droned on about the skyline, the history, the culture, the *ale* and the *scotch*. Was this really the same person as the smug bastard he'd heard on the radio? Russell had matched the syrupy drawl to an image of pumped-up, American meatloaf. In the pale, underdeveloped flesh, Fox gulped his words as if he didn't care for them much himself.

—People always want to know about a writer's background, where they come from and all. Well, see, my mother had been planning to accompany me on this trip but Pa got sick with some bug and so she couldn't make it. Ma was really looking forward to visiting your country so before I start on the book, I'd like to read you one of her letters. That way she'll kinda be here in spirit.

Dear Son,
I'm real sorry you couldn't make it up here for Thanksgiving. We had a fresh snowfall and everything was real pretty. When I go out back for firewood and see the trees all fluffy like they're wearing white fur coats I feel just like I'm in that song, Walking in a Winter Wonderland. *But lord it's cold out and tricky getting around. I've cooked up all your pa's favourite dinners and packed them in the freezer. Berta says she'll drop by during the day* – Berta's my sister – *and he and Johnny* – my Uncle Johnny,

folks – *have planned card games for a couple of evenings so Pa won't be too lonesome. I guess the house will look like a chicken coop when I get home but heck, I want him to have a good time too.*

It's just so exciting. Scotland! I bought me a new winter coat which I just love. It's a kinda rustic look, forest green wool with a cute little tartan trim on the cuffs and pockets. I've read my guide book twice already and marked a whole buncha places of interest. I've been reading up about the olden times too. Was it all that history made you set your book about fruit in Scotland?

—I don't get this, Rusty.

—Neither do I.

Fox coughed several times and leafed through a copy of his book until his quivering fingers settled on a page.

—Okay . . . now I'm going to read you a passage from my novel, *Eating Passionfruit in Bed*. This title has just come out in paperback over here and the bookshop, my publisher and I would be real pleased if you'd buy as many copies as you can carry home.

Fox got a bit of a laugh out of his sales pitch and beamed as if he'd been given a standing ovation.

—It's about a guy who's drawn into a brief but intense relationship with a woman who kinda loves the guy she lives with but finds . . . difficult.

Difficult? Difficult? He wasn't the one who was *riddled with dissatisfaction.* If Muriel could drink air, Russell could be selectively deaf. Fill the head up with other words, don't hear the drivel drifting across the heads of the audience like a bad smell; any words, just block out the voice, keep the inner soundtrack rolling, not so hard, easy really, one word after another . . .

'But one night was all he had; the next day he would be gone from this two-bit city and to live life wishing for what might have been was not his style. The day — the night — was for seizing. Iona had wasted herself on dead wood for so long but he would make up for it, tear those drab years from her memory, like the curled yellowed pages of an old calendar, light the fire he knew smouldered deep inside her . . .'

And then he fucked her. Then Guy Rightman fucked Iona Rivers, Fox fucked Arlene. Arlene got fucked and he, the blameless one, got well and truly shafted. *It just happened*: Arlene. He wasn't going to listen to another word. There were only so many minutes Fox could inflict his crap on the audience, only so many minutes before they'd get restless or thirsty or stiff, or need to take a leak, a finite time, a very short time really and as he'd read the whole bloody lot already, more than once, and that passage in particular, he knew it well enough, did not need to hear it again, did not want to hear it again, the thing to do was keep on blocking the bugger until he'd run out of slush about Arlene's mystical attractions, not that it mattered now, not that it meant a fucking thing now. Arlene was of no more interest to him than a character in a novel, a novel he'd given up reading.

Russell's symptoms: denial, denial, denial

Applause. More beaming from Fox.

—Squishy, said Muriel.

The rest of the audience was politely appreciative. When the applause finally clapped itself out, Green Blouse bustled to the fore again, thanked everybody for everything and asked for questions. At the front, a hand shot up.

—Mr Fox, is your novel based on personal experience?

Fox put down his book, rocked on his heels and relaxed a fraction. He knew this question. Russell knew that he knew this question. And had prepared an answer.

—Partly, but never the part you think.

There was a confused but expectant lull as the audience attempted to work out what the author meant. From the street, Russell could hear Imelda howling. Muriel, diverted by the dog, was blowing kisses at the window.

—Ask your question, Rusty. We don't have long. Imelda's eaten her sweeties.

Russell shook his head.

—What's wrong with you, boy? You got cold toes?

—Feet, he croaked. Cold feet.

—Toes, feet, who cares.

Even if he'd wanted to speak, he wouldn't have been able to make himself heard. A clamp had closed over the bridge of his nose, pinching the narrow channels of his sinuses. His throat was on fire.

Muriel stuck her hand in the air and stood on tiptoe.

—Excuse me! This story you wrote.

—Yes? said Fox.

—What's it for? I mean apart from maybe getting some of your readers hot and horny, what's it for?

Chairs creaked in collective animation as half the audience turned to see who had asked the awkward question. Fox blinked, stepped back and bumped into the bookshelves. The more Russell looked at the man, the more he was reminded, not of all-time winner Guy Rightman, but of the *more to be pitied than despised* Leslie Little.

—I . . . ah . . . don't know if I've ever been asked that

question before. And . . . ah . . . don't rightly know if I can answer it.

—Well, could you try? said Muriel.

—I really need to think about that question. If you'd ah, like to wait behind after the ah, signing session, I'd sure try my best to . . . give you an explanation.

—I don't want an explanation, said Muriel. You ask a question, you want an answer, right?

Green Blouse stepped forward decisively.

—Any other questions?

—Ask, Rusty. Ask your goddamn question.

—Let's go. Let's just go.

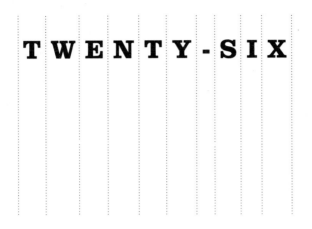

TWENTY-SIX

Peanuts

Sleet blew into Russell's eyes, causing the fairy lights strung on the trees across the street to pulse blearily and the carousel horses to blur into revolving bands of colour. Imelda, crunching something between her teeth, eyed them both reproachfully and unpicked her paws from the slushy pavement one by one.

—Poor baby. Am I the worst mother in the world?

Muriel slapped the sleet off Imelda's back, took off her scarf, began to rub down the dog with it and smother her with babytalk. Seeing all the attention the dog was getting, Russell felt a vague pang of something resembling jealousy.

—Spare change?

Russell wiped his eyes and looked round.

—Not you again.

—Small world, man.

—Yeah. How're you doing?

—Slim pickings the night. You'd think in shite weather folk would be more generous but it works the other way, man.

As well as his ancient coat and Russell's cast-off fleece, Peter was sporting a hand-tooled leather stetson and lilac satin trainers. In spite of the cold, he bounced jauntily from one foot to the other, in a combined attempt to keep warm and check out the passers-by. There weren't many: the streets were very quiet and the few folk who'd braved the weather were hunched up, insulated against elemental and human intrusion.

—Been at the book do? Have them all the time in there. At a number of other venues, n'all. If you can find somewhere to spruce up beforehand, you can get a free bevvy down you every night of the week. A few I know have got the visiting speakers gigs down to a fine art. The trick is to fill up and nick out just before they introduce the guest.

Peter jerked a thumb at Muriel and grinned.

—That your bird?

—I'm nobody's bird, sonny! Muriel spat back at him. And what exactly were you feeding my dog?

—Salted peanuts, said Peter. Lot of protein in nuts.

—Lot of goddamn salt in them too.

—Well, I didn't have any dry roast to hand.

—If my dog gets sick, I'm gonna come looking for you.

—Listen, doll . . .

—Doll! Doll! I'm nobody's goddamn doll!

Russell felt it was necessary to intervene.

—Peter, this is Muriel. Muriel, Peter . . .

—Well, listen here, *Muriel*, if you leave your dog out in the fucking snow it's gonna get sick, salted peanuts or no. I should know. Mate of mine died the other night.

Hypothermia. Happens all the time once the cold weather sets in. And who gives a monkey's?

—Sorry, said Muriel, but we've all got problems staying alive.

—Did you get that room you were after? Russell asked Peter.

—Room?

Peter's gaze drifted down the long, straight, empty street.

—Last time I saw you, you were going to look for a room . . .

—Was I? You needing a room, like? I've got somewhere for the night but it's a bit cramped . . .

—No, no, said Russell. I'm fine.

—And women aren't allowed, more's the fucking pity . . . Got the time, man? Got to watch my time.

Bobby's Rolex was still making a cold, heavy lump in Russell's pocket.

—Here, he said, handing Peter the watch. This'll keep you right.

—Aw hey, now that's some timepiece, man. These things cost money!

—Do what you like with it.

Peter held Bobby's watch up to the light.

—Nice. Very nice. Ta, mate. Ta very much. Sure you don't need a room? Was that bird not trying to chuck you out?

—Not her, somebody else.

Peter nodded slowly, glanced at Muriel and grinned again and lowered his voice.

—So that's the new edition? Somebody's a fast worker.

—Say no more, eh?

—My lips are sealed.

Accompanied by a blast of warm air, three serious young women hurried through the automatic doors of the bookshop, buttoning coats and pulling on gloves. Peter spun on the tips of his luminous trainers and stretched out a hand but the trio scurried off down the street where a string quartet – lasses with flowing locks and winning smiles – emerged from a shop doorway and burst into an up-tempo version of 'Summertime'.

—Students, said Peter. Paying their way through college. My competition, he added, without malice.

Muriel and the dog were glaring impatiently at Russell.

—Time you fucked off, said Peter. You're losing me business, mate, hanging around here, cramping my style.

The deserted park was like a black and white negative, the sky dark, ground and trees pale, the scratchy blanket of dead grass transformed into a pristine downie, the trees furred with crystals. Even on the footpath their own muffled steps were the first. The dog trotted ahead, her tail casting a powdery arc in her wake.

—Dumb dog, said Muriel.

—She's happy.

—I know, said Muriel. I'm just jealous.

She shivered, stamped her feet. Russell put his arm round her but she removed it.

—That won't help, Rusty.

—Will it do any harm?

—What have you been telling that person, Rusty?

—Nothing, he lied. Nothing at all.

—Where I come from, careless talk costs lives.

—I know, said Russell. I know.

—You know shit, said Muriel.

They walked on in icy silence for a long time.

—I miss the night market; pottering about the stalls. I miss the smells, all twisting through each other like coloured threads. Sometimes I used to close my eyes and let myself be led by the nose to fruit, flowers, spices. Not so nice in the rainy season: in the rainy season the market is just stinky. And I miss hearing flowers open up after a rainstorm.

— You can't hear flowers open.

—Yes you can, Rusty. In my country you can, if you listen hard enough you can hear the petals stretching out to welcome the sun.

—Maybe you're homesick.

—Homesick is bullshit.

—It's healthy to miss home a bit.

—Don't talk to me about healthy.

—I don't mean your body.

—You telling me it's healthy to feel bad?

—No, what I'm saying is . . . Christ it's nothing to do with me . . .

—You're goddamn right, boy. And I am not homesick, okay? And this is not going to be our first fight.

—Tell me about your husband, said Russell.

—What about him?

—How did you meet him?

—In a bar, Rusty. A sleazy bar in Manila for foreigners and local pimps.

—Doesn't sound like your sort of place.

—I didn't have a lot of choice where I hung out around that time. Okay so getting hitched to a jerk who wanted a housemaid and sex worker rolled into one was a pain but it could have been worse for me, Rusty, a lot worse. Things were very tricky for all of us girls who'd been campaigning for a fair election, all of us who hadn't already been butchered by the death squads.

The smiling, blacked-out faces: the targets.

—Marrying a foreigner was the only way I could get out of the country. At every step of the way I was sure something must go wrong. Even on the plane, waiting for take-off, I was ready for the president's men to storm down the aisle and blow me to bits as I sat beside my new husband. I was so dumb. My husband had connections. Fingers in all kinds of pies. And he brought me to Scotland. I thought that maybe sometime I'd try to track down my old man . . .

—And did you?

—No. Don't even know whether he's alive or dead. At first I was too busy cooking and cleaning for my good-for-nothing husband and then, I dunno, once he pissed off I had to find a job and a place to live . . . I kind of forgot about it, I guess.

Muriel dug her hands into her pockets and stared ahead of her.

—I don't want to talk any more. I got it out of my chest now.

—*Off* your chest.

—I say out, I mean out, okay?

—Okay, Muriel, okay. Out it is.

Snow was falling steadily as they turned into Russell's street. On the opposite pavement, a group of women in saris clustered under a speckled streetlight, umbrellas held high. Frothy swirls of rose, jade, sapphire and tangerine glowed in the lamp's diffuse beam. Bracelets flashed and clinked, beads rattled, voices rose and dipped in light, musical chatter, spilling into the night. Even Imelda seemed impressed. Her huffs and grunts gave way to an almost ladylike sigh. One of the women was waving energetically; eventually Russell realised that the sparkling creature across the road was Mrs Ramasawmy from Nice Price.

—What's the occasion? he asked.

—My niece graduation. Going to be accountant. CA. Then actuary. Good money.

Mrs Ramasawmy turned to her friends and switched back to animated Hindi. A brief peal of giggles was stifled by the tinny clink of many bracelets. Russell followed Muriel and Imelda along the street. The dog had cheered up; she snapped at snowflakes and pissed copiously over the thin rime of frost which glazed the pavement.

—D'you want to stay the night?

—No.

Muriel had splashed off down the street, Imelda scritching at the back window. He'd invited her to stay. She'd declined his invitation. Flatly refused it. Fair enough, she didn't need him piling on the pressure. But she'd let him into her life a little bit and pushed her way into his . . . Why hadn't he tried to persuade her to stay? She might have responded to a bit more effort on his part. Did she assume that sex would be obligatory? Did she not want sex with him, tonight or any subsequent night? Was that enjoyable interlude – the only enjoyable interlude recently – over and done with already? The fishy hallway and the living room weren't what anybody would call enticing but he'd have changed the sheets and found a bulb for the bedside lamp with the pink concertina skirt which, apparently, had failed the style challenge for Boon's. If he'd had time, he might have looked out something to cover the marks left by Arlene's prints of tumescent vegetables.

Why had Muriel come to visit? He'd been too taken up

with his own pitiful preoccupations and hadn't even thought to ask. Or even to ask why she'd rushed off and left him the other morning. Anyway, she'd gone back to her rat-infested cottage, didn't want whatever it was he had to offer. The last thing Muriel seemed to want was any kind of protection. In the event of a showdown, she'd be the one who'd be doing the fending off. He could just see her, hands on hips, in the big jersey, the muddy wellies, screaming abuse into the still country air. Or, like one of those steely grannies in spaghetti westerns, striding into the yard, strong sunlight casting deep shadows across her face as she raised the gun to her shoulder, squinted down the sights and blasted any intruder to kingdom come. Why didn't she have a bloody phone? A mobile. Something. Some link with the outside world. Why hadn't he tried harder to persuade her to stay?

Russell's symptoms: exclusion, irrelevance, self-pity, the unfamiliar ache of loneliness

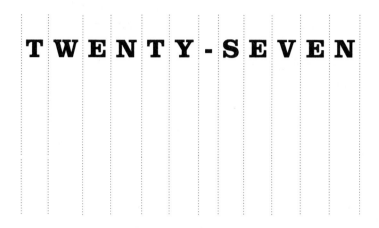

TWENTY-SEVEN

Love Nest

In spite of the snow continuing to fall – or perhaps because of it – the Grassmarket was teeming with folk. Throngs of rowdy youngsters slithered around the streets, trooped in or out of the pubs, queued outside the chip shop and the crêpe stall or pelted each other with snowballs. Footsore, out-of-season tourists, bemused by the street life and unsure whether to risk the local watering holes, contented themselves with flash photos – backside of castle with snow on battlements, Covenanters' Memorial, dosser in tartan blanket with transistor radio. Window shopping, too, offered an eclectic mixture of the twee, the trendy and the total tatt: from retro rag-store fashion to ball gowns, from joke shops to jewellers, all of it was bathed in a seductive seasonal glow.

Though he lived only ten minutes' walk away, Russell's neighbourhood had none of the buzz of the Grassmarket. If he moved, *when* he moved – there was no *if* about it any more: the only questions were *when*, *where to*, and *what could he afford?* – a flat in a livelier area might be the thing, though property prices in the city centre were going through the roof. A new international tourist hotel had been thrown up in the middle of all the quaint, historic premises of the area. It was an ideal tourist location, if you were a few floors up from street level and double-glazed windows reduced the noise. You wouldn't need to go out at all to soak up the atmosphere. Maybe Fox had booked in there, charmed by the associations of the past and the exuberant street life of the present. Maybe he and Arlene were over there at that very moment, catching up on lost time . . .

—People always sit at the window when they come to visit. Don't know why I bothered decorating really. All anybody ever looks at is the view.

Reluctantly Russell turned his back on the view from Todd's fourth-floor window and attempted to take an interest in Todd's décor. He had, after all, invited himself up on the spur of the moment. The least he could do was try to pay attention to what he was being told, though after five years with Arlene, he had an aversion to domestic accessories. Still, Todd's living room was impressive. A small room with a low ceiling, liberal use of mirrors, subtle lighting, a minimum of furniture – low-slung couch, lacquered coffee table – it gave the impression of space and comfort. Arlene would have been asking for the address of his suppliers.

—You haven't been here for years, man. Come and see what I've done with the rest of the place.

A guided tour of Todd's flat hadn't been on Russell's mind when he'd buzzed the intercom. What had been on his mind as he'd stood, whisky bottle in hand and desperate to get out of the cold, was that he couldn't think of anyone else to visit. Arlene had reminded him recently – with regard to Muriel – that he didn't have any women friends. The truth was that he didn't really have any men friends either. Mates at work and blokes in the local pubs he'd happily prop up the bar with, he'd never felt a lack of those – but actual friends? He'd moved around a bit, of course, small hops from one town to another, one plant to another. There was always a big enough work-force for him to find one or two amenable cronies.

—I never cook unless I've got company, and even then, I'm happy to skip the food-as-foreplay routine. But a decent kitchen works like a charm on women. Todd's kitchen could have been lifted straight out of a magazine – all steel and slate, marble and waxed wood. Not only was it ludicrously flash, it was also spotless. Arlene, for one, would have asked to move in. Apart from the whisky bottle, the only thing on the crud-free work tops was a bowl of phallic-shaped gourds.

—You don't actually eat these things, do you?

—Nah, they're hollow, just husks. People make maracas from them, fill them with beans or something, I don't know. They do have other, more interesting applications, of course. By the way, Fairley, I'm expecting somebody. But you're all right for an hour or so.

Russell should have known the minute he came in that Todd had a date. The crisp jeans and expensively simple linen shirt were fresh on. He was newly shaved and expensively scented, judging by the bottles on the black glass shelf in the bathroom. Nobody hung around their home spruced up like that for no reason.

—That shower unit cost more than the rest of the fitments put together. Ten different settings, from the barest tickle to the force of a fireman's hose. Worth every penny.

What in God's name was he doing here, feigning interest in Todd's bathroom, his hallway, study? He wanted to talk to somebody about Muriel, Arlene, Fox, about homeless Peter and dead Bobby, about how wretched he felt when Muriel drove off and left him on his doorstep, staring at the marks her tyres had left in the slush.

—Arlene working late again, is she?

—Mmmnn . . .

Todd smirked.

—Must be a pain, her working nights all the time.

What the fuck was he thinking about? Talk to Todd about Muriel, Arlene?

—. . . And last but certainly not least . . . Is this not the business, man?

Todd flung open the door to his bedroom. Russell took in the king-sized four-poster with its filmy drapes, satin sheets and a bank of matching pillows. Apart from a steel coat stand, naked except for Todd's bathrobe dripping off one of its vicious-looking hooks, whatever else the room contained was stashed away in built-in cupboards. As in the living room, strategic use of mirrors had been made.

—I'd have thought a four-poster was a bit old-fashioned for you, Todd.

—No, no, that's something the good old days got right. Curtains add a bit of mystique. And bedposts come in handy.

When the guided tour was finally over, they returned to the living room. In his allotted hour with Todd, Russell managed to avoid any further mention of Arlene or Muriel. Instead, he reported in detail on Bobby's funeral, the only safe topic he could think of but clearly one in which Todd was less than interested. Russell was aware of drinking too fast. Todd, as he told Russell smugly, was saving himself for later.

—D'you ever think about death, Todd? I mean do you ever worry that you might have something seriously wrong with you, possibly terminal, and you might not find out until it's too late?

—Fucksake, man . . . You should steer clear of funerals.

Both of them stared out of the window. Todd had anticipation in his eyes. For a weekday, it was late for a date although Russell didn't expect Todd wasted much time on preliminaries and given some of Todd's likely options, not so late after all. A girl from the saunas doing home delivery, a waitress he'd tipped excessively? The intercom buzzed in the hall. Todd went to answer it, his voice deepening to a schmoozy purr. He returned with Russell's half-empty bottle.

—I'd invite you to stay, man, but on this occasion, three's a crowd. Take the whisky away with you. All I need for tonight is on its way up. Sorry not to have more time to spare. Just leave the door open.

They came face to face with each other on the second-floor landing.

—Well, hello there! God – these stairs! The last time I came up here I had to rest halfway. But what a coincidence running into you! I was just thinking about your interesting situation the other day and wondering how things were shaping up.

Germaine Shuck, solicitor from the works' firm of Anglesey and Hope, stood on Todd's stair and smiled brightly. There was no question about where she was going, no question at all. Like Todd, she was tarted up for a date.

Suede jacket, little black dress, high-heeled boots, the hair freshly brushed and flowing, the lipstick glossy, the evening perfume distinctly more sexy than her daytime choice. Russell felt sick.

—I'm fine, he muttered. Everything's fine.

—Pleased to hear it. Well, bye, Mr Fairley, enjoy your night.

Russell took the remainder of the stairs two at a time, and, in spite of the printed message requesting that the door was closed quietly on entering and leaving, slammed it behind him.

Russell started up the slippery steps of the Vennel, slugging from his bottle and cursing Todd to the snow-filled sky. Todd knew. The smirk when he asked whether Arlene was working late; that was no innocent little question. Todd fucking knew. And Russell knew who'd told him. After the guided tour of Todd's love nest, he could picture the moment of realisation in revoltingly clear detail: Germaine Shuck, gazing post-coitally at the ceiling while Todd went to fetch the remains of the Cava, Germaine Shuck, luxuriating under the downie, her eager brain clicking into gear, belatedly putting the name to the face and blurting out the fascinating recollection.

How much had the woman said and how much had Todd already passed on? How far had it spread? Was it already too late to nip the story in the bud before it replicated itself, mutated and invaded all strata of the staff? Had his private humiliation already become plant property, to be sniggered over along with the tits in the tabloids? Like an airborne virus, gossip was rapid, indiscriminate, crossed all social boundaries . . .

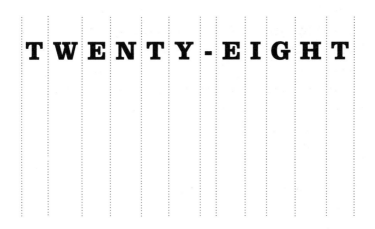

TWENTY-EIGHT

Bad Blood

There was an absence of the usual subterranean rumblings, an unnatural hush for which Russell was grateful. Still groggy from too much whisky the night before and too many nagging thoughts which had kept him in a state of irate semi-consciousness all night, a bit of peace and quiet might give him a chance to recover. He'd lain awake trying to work out how best to deal with the unwanted awareness that Todd, for one, had inside information on him. There were only two ways of dealing with such a situation. One was to ignore it altogether in the hope that it would fade away, the other was to grovel to Todd, beg him to keep what he knew about *Eating Passionfruit in Bed* to himself. It was unthinkable to grovel to Todd. Russell had seen others do it, in the past. It brought out the worst in the man.

In the changing rooms, rubber boots stood in rows and white oversuits hung limply from their pegs. Clearly, production had been stopped. This in itself was normal enough. During the course of the renovations there had been the occasional hiccup, electrical problems mostly, which had brought the plant to a temporary standstill but a personally signed missive from Everett, requesting all personnel to report to their supervisors on arrival, was rare.

Russell passed the new sterile unit – still unfinished – a vacant steel and glass cube, lit up from inside, glowing and gleaming like a futuristic shrine. For weeks he'd passed it and seen work going on, finicky patient work, precision soldering, microscopic measurements. It was an impressive little spectacle, this new, improved space, public in the sense that its contents could be seen by all but exclusive too, a state-of-the-art, environmentally regulated cell. A germ-free atmosphere. Approximately. Try as they might, there was always an infinitesimal percentage of the buggers which sneaked through every trap.

Instead of going straight to Todd's office, as instructed, which, after last night, he was in no hurry to do, no bloody hurry at all, he nipped into the lift, pressed the button for the second floor and savoured a few brief moments of solitude. He'd seen a TV documentary about people who were obsessed by lifts and spent hours every day going up and down in them, not letting anyone else in. At the time he'd thought they were bonkers but today he could see their point. Privacy was a hard thing to find in this world, as was a sense of purpose. His scratched reflection in the steel door was as indistinct and fuzzed at the edges as he felt. You were supposed to grow into yourself as you got older, that was the theory, but did that mean growing into more of a blur than you'd been at the beginning? Science claimed to be about precision, sharp edges, clear routes between a and b, about definitions and distinctions, about clarity. But wasn't it just another fumbling about in the dark, hoping a light would come on somewhere and a path would miraculously open up, leading to the end of the tunnel? Wasn't it just another kind of made-up story?

He didn't want to speak to Muriel, not here, not now, just to know whether or not she'd come to work. He'd just take a look through the windows of the lab then go, as requested, and report to Todd. The glass panels on the lab doors were blacked out with tape: TESTS IN PROGRESS. AUTHORISED ACCESS ONLY. Bugger it. The one time he was interested in the bloody labs and he couldn't even peek through the windows because something private, something exclusive was going on.

—Ah, Fairley. I was hoping to catch you today.

Morris Morrison's youthful face widened into what Russell took to be a smile. The works' doctor had sneaked up and caught him hanging about the labs for no good reason, and certainly none that he'd admit to Morris. Or anybody else, except the person he wanted to see, though he wasn't entirely sure why he wanted to see Muriel in the first place. Getting mixed up with a woman at work and one with an ex-husband into the bargain who, for all he knew, might appear out of the murk and reclaim his wife . . .

—What's up now?

—Oh, well . . . I am cognisant of a small proportion of the possibilities but the director has imposed a strict procedural code on all communications today, so really, I'm not at liberty to comment.

It was too early in the day for long sentences.

—But as I said, on another matter, I was hoping to catch you . . .

—Spit it out, man.

—Yes, yes. Concerning the blood sample I took from you last week . . . well, I'd like another one. Nothing at all to worry about. I'd just like to double-check a couple of things. Maybe you could step into the office?

—Can I do it later? I'm supposed to go straight to see Todd.

—Well, I suppose later today would do. With the plant shut down, I expect you'll have some time to kill.

—I can think of better ways to kill it.

—I'm sure you can.

Morris renewed flexing his facial muscles and flattening the pockets of his tweed jacket. Russell could picture him at sixty: heavier about the middle, redder about the cheeks, eyelids ridged like oyster shells, still patting his pockets, tugging at the collar of a crisp striped shirt and sweeping back a boyish squall of silver hair.

Russell hoped Morris wouldn't notice the inconsistency in his being on the second floor when he was supposed to be in the basement.

There was a distinct sense of drama in the zapped, disinfected air, a tense, heavy silence as if, in a soundproof room nearby, something troublesome was being smothered. When Russell arrived at his appointed destination, Todd stopped pacing the room and glanced pointedly at his watch. It was only a few minutes past nine, the plant was shut down . . .

—Well, it's finally happened, said Todd. All those years with a clean slate blown to fuck.

—What's up?

—Can't say.

—Because you don't know or because you're not allowed to?

—Bit of both.

—God.

—God's got fuck all to do with it.

—What then?

—I told you, Fairley. I'm under orders. And the giver of orders is not, today, the most rational of individuals.

—How bad are we talking about, man?

—I expect that depends on your point of view.

—Christ, man, you can tell me, can't you? It'll come out soon enough, won't it?

—What will?

—I don't know, do I, because you're keeping me in the dark.

—We're all in the fucking dark, Fairley. Follow me.

As Russell followed Todd along the corridor, hearing his leather-soled Italian shoes squeaking expensively, he realised that, though they'd both worked in the plant for years, there was nothing resembling a bond between them, no affinity, not even the faintest suggestion of loyalty. Though they were part of the same process, the same production line, that was it.

Todd's unwillingness to spill the beans was enough to convince Russell that something pretty bloody serious had gone wrong and something serious had only one explanation: bad blood. Bad blood which had somehow slipped through the screening and, in the form of one or other product, been sent out. And used? If the cause was something they didn't test for, like a new viral strain, the plant might not be liable. They couldn't test for every pathogen. Well, they could, if unlimited funds were available but, like everywhere else, there was the budget to consider. Blood was a business after all, not yet out on the open market but possibly going that way. If voluntary supplies ran out, they'd be at the mercy of the market and who chooses to sell their blood? Not the upright, responsible donors who do it for the greater good, who want to contribute something to society, in this case their own erythrocytes, leukocytes and thrombocytes. It wouldn't be that sector of the community who'd queue up for a few quid but desperate folk, folk who couldn't get hold of the dosh any other way.

From the veins of a donor to the self-seal plasma bag, to the batch of slush puppy sliding down the chute. Cold ethanol fractionation to extract proteins. Purification by means of advanced chromatography, ultrafiltration and freeze-drying. Bottling, boxing, the deep-freeze. From the deep-freeze to the refrigerated vans, to hospitals, health centres and pharmacies, to the bloodstream of a grateful patient . . .

For years you get up in the morning day after day and the routine's the same, predictable, boring but reliable. You know where you are – or where you should be – and what's to be done with the time ahead. A simple sequence of non-events keeps lives and livelihoods ticking over, a set of orders, rules and restrictions. Timetables and time limits, checks and double checks keep the process on course, the products rolling off the conveyor belt. On a day when Russell had been looking forward to the familiar monotony, it had been denied him.

—Where are we going?

—Where do you think? The press pariahs haven't got wind of anything yet but when they do, who's going to give a toss about our past virginal record? Everett's keen to stall the story. Which is where you come in.

—Me?

—Aye, Fairley. You.

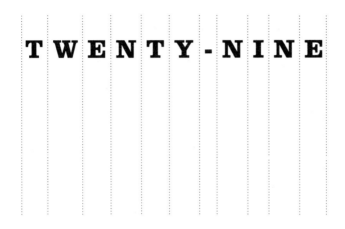

T W E N T Y - N I N E

The Free Lunch

Ostentatious floral arrangements, the gleam of oiled wood, marble, regularly Windowlened glass and the low-key decorations – all muted red and dusty gold – had an instantly sedating effect. In between the fake trees decked out with tartan bows, an exhibition of African wood carvings gleamed darkly. Sleek curvaceous heads, torsos and entwined figures had been chiselled from lumps of ebony and mahogany. A few of the pieces already had SOLD stickers on their astronomical price tags. Somebody must be making a nice little living exploiting African artists while outside the door, on the far side of the square, the bronze statue of a Winnie Mandela look-alike standing with an arm around the shoulder of a skinny child had yet again been smeared with white paint. Erected during the Free Nelson era it had been vandalised on a regular basis; these days, though, it wasn't always clear which side of the race ticket was doing the daubing.

—Sorry to drag you into town like this but your director didn't seem keen on an *in situ* interview. Why not?

—Renovations going on at the moment. Upgrading. Everywhere's at sixes and sevens.

—I see. Jackie Frost, by the way. I haven't eaten here for ages so I can't tell you what's worth having.

Renovations. If pneumonia was one of the symptoms, airborne bacteria could have been the cause of the infection. With so much building work on the go, the earth disturbed and throwing up hitherto dormant microbes by the million . . .

Rehashing the story about Bobby had struck Russell as a cock-eyed idea but Everett had been convinced – insistent, in fact, doggedly insistent – that it might, for a while, deflect media attention from the real story about to break in all its possible implications behind the blacked-out doors of the lab.

The waiter was hovering. A sombre young man with a wide brow and big, moist eyes, he nodded minimally as Jackie Frost ordered for both of them, then retreated as smoothly as if he were on well-oiled castors. Jackie Frost shook her head. The woman had narrow, hazel eyes and a long curved jaw, like a hammer.

—Not a lot of life in him, eh? Talking of which, the man who died after his spell in the icebox, Robert Doyle . . .

—He didn't die immediately, said Russell. He came round. When I saw him in hospital he seemed to be making good enough progress . . .

Bobby's hands turning the dials, tightening connections,

*his tobacco-brown teeth, the rasp of his breathing as he
concentrated all his attention on carrying out Russell's
instructions, his mumbling doubts about the wisdom of
doing so, the seconds clicking away . . .*

—You went to visit him. So you were close?
—No.
—But you went to visit him in hospital. People don't go
and visit just anybody in hospital.
—I'd . . . saved his life, well, I thought I had. That's been
in the papers already. It's old news.
—The man was alive. Now he's dead. And you are my
only living link. So tell me what you know.

—*Say it again, Fairley,* Everett had said. *Slowly. Spin out
the answers. Mr Doyle is, after all, no longer with us, so a
little embellishment, a little elaboration on the human
interest aspect couldn't do any harm to anyone, could it?
Let me worry about the possible benefits of your jaunt
downtown. It's what I'm paid for, unfortunately.*

—A good bloke, Bobby. Friendly, helpful, solitary but
you would be if you worked at night. I mean, there's not
much opportunity for a normal social life if you're clocking on when everybody else is clocking off . . .
Jackie Frost had an annoying habit of scraping a fingernail across her scalp, hooking a strand of her heavy reddish
hair and twirling it as she listened impatiently until Russell
said something she decided was worth scribbling on her
notepad. Which wasn't much, by the looks of it.
—So you mean he wasn't normal?
—I mean he worked unsociable hours. Who can pick
and choose these days?

The hair scraped back, the pencil rasping against paper. Russell was suprised – and relieved – that she didn't have a dictaphone. When the food arrived she elbowed her note-pad aside and began slicing up her crispy chicken strips and drizzling dressing on her salad.

Drizzling: an Arlene word. Arlene had a special jug for *drizzling* olive oil over this, that and the next thing; a glass jug with a long spout, thin as a pipette. Had Arlene been with him, she'd have been quizzing him as to whether the sole in watercress sauce he'd ordered was better than Boon's. Meals out with Arlene, God, a busman's holiday and no mistake. The Frost woman wasn't great to eat with either, spearing her meat and disposing of it greedily but without relish. But Arlene – he still couldn't make sense of her not showing up to meet the author. Had her feelings for Fox, after all, not been as overwhelming as those of Iona Rivers for Guy Rightman? Had *Eating Passionfruit in Bed* been less an earth-moving experience and more a spitting out of pips? Did Fox, after all, have something resembling an imagination?

—So. Mr Doyle, said Jackie.

Not having a gaffer breathing down your neck must have been a freedom of sorts but night-watchman at the plant was a lonely job. But maybe that itself had been part of the problem: too much responsibility, isolation, free-dom. Maybe it wasn't good for people to be left to their own devices, fantasies, weaknesses. Maybe if somebody kept an eye on you, reminded you not to let things slip too far, you kept an eye on yourself too, kept yourself in check. Who knows? And what did he really know about Bobby?

—Did Mr Doyle have a grudge against the boss?

—I don't think so. No more than anybody else, anyway.

—So your boss is a bastard?

—All I'm saying is that the boss is the obvious target for complaints. Comes with the salary, doesn't it?

The filter . . . had he remembered to check the filter?

—Hmmm. So, was Mr Doyle politically active?
—Not that I know of.
—Capable of sabotage?

—He wasn't capable of much when I found him.
—Could he, for example, have turned off the deep freeze on purpose?
—I doubt it. Anyway, where's the motive?
—So . . . home life? What was Mr Doyle's home life like?

How could he possibly know what the man's home life was like? Apart from the hospital visit and the night Russell had been on call, he and Bobby had never had anything resembling a conversation.

Even with the elaborate filtration system, something airborne could have got through via the air-conditioning. There was always a small chance and if the filter in the freeze-dryer had been faulty and he'd hadn't checked it . . . Christ, had he forgotten to check the filter? He could barely remember anything from that night, except that, after all the moping and cursing over Arlene, the taxi bumping up the drive, the strip lights humming and flickering and giving him a blinding headache, he was in no fit state to be there.

Jackie Frost had finished her chicken strips and was waiting for an answer.
—Bobby was single. No dependants. That's all I know.

—Oh come on. Your boss wouldn't have sent you to talk to me if you didn't know a bit more about the man.

Oh yes he would. Everett would have sent along a talking parrot if he'd thought it might help.

—I work in a big place. It can take years to get to know anything personal about folk who work there. And Bobby being on night shift as well . . .

—I work in a big place too, Mr Fairley. And I know a hell of a lot about my colleagues.

—It's your job to dig into folk's business. Mine isn't nearly so . . . personal.

In a way, though, it was; it might not offer the kind of imbroglio that Jackie Frost was keen to get her teeth into but when it came down to it, blood was about as personal as you could get. Blood carried the indelible stamp of the past and was in many ways an accurate barometer for the future. Blood, the endless journey, the ongoing story; genetic saga, mystery thriller, modern romance, social realism, science fiction. Blood picked you out, nailed you down. Blood could damn you or save you. Blood was the ultimate witness. *Sample for Morris. By the end of the day. Nothing to worry about. At this point. Double-check a couple of things. What things?* What was the story of his blood?

Something outside had caught the reporter's attention. The hotel overlooked a small square with a frozen pond and a defunct fountain. Where an open space and a view of the city's soot-seasoned Georgian pride had previously been available to diners, an office block in the throes of construction was, floor by floor, eating up the outlook. A massive crane swung a sheaf of metal rods across the square and deposited them in the shaft of the unfinished erection.

—Amazing, she said, blinking herself into wide-eyed

astonishment. I've got a real thing about cranes; that guy sitting up there in his wee cabin controlling that massive load. Take a look at that load. That's art . . . God . . . espresso, time for espresso.

—I'd better be getting back to work, said Russell.

—Well, I'll just have to have my *café solo* and fantasise about the crane driver. Must be something to do with danger. Seen that crazy stunt man on the telly that drives cars over gorges, the one with eyes like lasers?

Jackie Frost's own eyes were glazing over. She tugged absently at her necklace. A string of beads no bigger than lentils wound round her neck several times and gathered in a loose knot at her throat. As the loaded cradle of the crane made another ponderous lurch above the square, the necklace broke and the liberated beads bounced and pittered over the remains of her lunch.

She unwound the remainder of the necklace and tossed it into the ashtray.

—Cheap shit, said Jackie. Made in Taiwan or the Philippines, I expect.

T H I R T Y

The Lives and Loves of Rods, Spirals and Spheres

—Ah'll see ye.

—Ye're no gonnae like it, man, believe me.

—Well, dinnae spin oot the agony. Turn the buggers over.

Jake flipped his cards over to reveal three sevens.

—Fucksake.

Davey clapped his hands to his pink, country-boy cheeks. Apologetically, Jake swept the winnings towards his corner.

—A big bairn, that's what Davey is, said Jake. Nae use at this game here. Nae use at aw. Ye've got tae huv a bit o deviousness in ye tae win at brag.

From the respective stakes, it was clear that Jake had cleaned up.

The delivery boys were hunkered down on a wooden

pallet. The overhanging roof of the packing house provided some shelter but, even so, it was a miserable windswept spot to pass the time.

—A dear way to pass your day, Davey, said Russell.

—It's the hands, man. Ah've had a run o duff hands.

—Me too, said Jake.

—Three sevens isnae a duff hand.

—Naw, said Jake. A fuck of a good one. Aw the rest was duff but the boy here didnae suss. If ah stuck on a pile, he'd cry off straight away. Cannae play brag withoot a bit deviousness, a bit brass neck in yer blood.

—Production still on hold? said Russell.

—Wid we be at the cairds if it wisnae? said Jake.

—Just asking.

—If this stoppage carries on too long, him and me'll no be speakin. Shame aboot Bobby Doyle, eh?

—Aye, said Jake. Efter Fairley here draggin the boy oot the jaws o death, they yawn again and swally him up. Makes ye think it's aw planned, dis it no? When your number's up, that's you, ken. Nae messin.

—Aye, said Davey. Maybe they Christian Scientists are right letting nature tak its coorse.

—Save a lot of money for the health service, said Russell.

—If we were aw Christian Scientists, said Jake, we wouldnae need a fuckin health service.

—No, said Davey. Nor this place neither.

The computer room was mobbed. Staff, minus their caps and masks, overalls and wellies, were lounging on the desks, sharing chairs and leaning against the walls. Though refreshments were restricted to coffee in Styrofoam cups and chocolate biscuits brought in from the dispenser in the cafeteria, the atmosphere was gloomily festive. Sadie and Myra, the women who'd been at Bobby's funeral, were bearing down on Hatcher, a sallow, oily-haired computer operator, who was introducing them to the Net.

—Cannae see why it's called surfin, said Myra. There's nae water.

Myra's thick red fingers clamped the man's insufficient shoulders.

—Gie's a deek at Patrick Swayze. Or Arnie. Let's get Arnie up there.

Hatcher clicked his mouse. Another page of text appeared.

—What's the use o that?

—Gimme a minute, ladies.

—Ye dinnae want tae read aboot em, ye want tae see em, in the flesh, aw brown and shiny, like basted turkeys.

—No the whole lot! said Sadie.

She folded her arms beneath the unconquerable ridge of her chest.

—Why no? said Myra. The lads get plenty tae goggle at.

—Aye, said Sadie, but if you ask me, some things are best kept for after dark.

—Right enough, said Myra. Ah've never seen a dick ah'd like tae huv sitting on ma mantelpiece.

None too comfortable with the way the conversation was going, Hatcher passed Myra the mouse, squirmed out of her clutches and joined the men at the next screen. A meaty scrum from the packing department, they were comparing league tables down the decades and arguing about the veracity of the information.

No sign of Todd. No sign of Muriel.

At reception, Dawn was on her swivel chair, listening to

someone on the other end of the telephone. With a gold-painted fingernail, she traced out tense little spirals in the air.

—Be with you in a minute, Mr Fairley.

She put her hand over the mouthpiece and made a *had-it-up-to-here* face.

Mid-afternoon and it was already dark outside. The blue test tube Madonna, lit up now, glowed eerily and drifted away from its base.

—Yes, yes, I can assure you that the director will be in touch at the earliest opportunity . . . No, I'm afraid he's otherwise engaged at the moment . . . Yes, I do realise that he's been a little difficult to get hold of today but the ongoing schedule of the plant is very demanding . . . As I've said, you are high on the waiting list . . . I quite agree that you should have priority status but there's really no more I can do for you at the moment . . . no, I'm afraid I can't put you through, I can't put anybody through. I'm very sorry you feel that way . . . Certainly. At the earliest opportunity. Bye. Thank you for calling. Absolutely. Bye. Yes. Bye. Bye.

—That sounded like hard work, said Russell.

—Some people just won't take no for an answer. So how can I help you, Mr Fairley? I'll tell you now, I don't think I've helped a single person today. I've tried, I've really tried but right now I'm not in the mood for doing any more trying. Everett's holed up through there and every flaming phonecall's an urgent request to speak to the boss. People can be so stubborn, you know. They hang on, chipping away, as if I'm the Berlin Wall or something. I know the Berlin Wall's been down for ever but you know what I mean. Get past the bird at reception and you're home – that's the attitude; I find it very stressful.

—Who's he in with?

Dawn spread her elbows and leaned forward. Her fluffy pink jersey caressed the stainless steel desk.

—That's the thing. Nobody. He's seen nobody since lunchtime and hasn't accepted a single call. It's not good for people to lock themselves away like that. A trouble shared is a trouble halved . . .

—In our line of work, it's more likely to be multiplied by the million.

—I suppose so, Mr Fairley. Oh dear. Well, feel free to try his door. There's absolutely no point in me buzzing him.

The Lives and Loves of Rods, Spirals and Spheres
Busy Bugs kill 17m around the world
Dithering Premier adds to Plague Panic
Professor Banned from Blood Centre
Former Prime Minister on Aids Charge
Britain to import blood plasma from America
'The best physic against the plague is to run away from it'

Every inch of Everett's bulletin board was covered with news clippings and quotations. Every item was numbered and dated. When an article was removed to make space for more recent information, it was added to the scrapbook — currently five volumes of immunological tidbits. In lieu of the usual wad of waiting-room magazines, Dawn had been instructed to offer the scrapbook to visitors along with the annual report. Basically, it was Everett's way of showing off: *Look at all these disasters, look at the calamities and catastrophes elsewhere, look at the horror stories, the nightmare scenarios, look what we have to contend with — devious bastards of microbes*

and devious bastards of men — look at the statistics, look at the
loopholes, the acts of God or the devil which throw up new
epidemics before you can say antigen, look at the safety records of
any other similar establishment. Then look at ours. Not that he'd
be saying that any more.

Russell watched the red light on the door brightening
and darkening. It had a steady pulse to it, like a heartbeat,
like blood pumping. He knocked again. Nothing. It was like
being back at school, quaking outside the heidie's door,
waiting to be summoned for punching Micky Murphy, for
making Micky Murphy's nose spout blood over the
playground, knowing that nothing he might say in his
defence could excuse what he'd done, nothing would help
him escape the lochgelly lying in wait for him in the middle
drawer of the heidie's desk, every second stretching inter-
minably until, from behind the door, the booming,
awesome voice bade him enter.

—Who is it?

Behind the closed door, Everett's voice squeaked thin
and high.

—It's Fairley, sir.

—Leave me alone!

—I'm just reporting back, Mr Everett. You asked me to
report back.

—I've changed my mind. I'm allowed to change my
mind. Leave me alone.

—Should I come back later?

—Who knows? said Everett. Who cares? I don't. I don't
care at all whether you come back or not. I can stop people
seeing me. I can cut them off. I can tell people to piddle off
and they'll go because I don't want to see them. I can keep
them waiting all day and all night and if I keep them waiting
long enough they'll stop trying, they will, eventually

they'll lose interest and find somebody else to get their teeth into, somebody else's blood to suck, somebody else to chew to shreds and spit out . . .

—Are you all right, sir?

—LEAVE ME ALONE!

THIRTY-ONE

Pest Maiden

Though he'd cleaned the car inside and out, traces of Arlene's perfume still hovered around the passenger seat. The inky sky was streaked with ice cloud. The wind knifed in, dislodging the light dusting of snow from the rooftops of cars, cracking the skin of frost on the windscreen. It was too cold a night to open the window for long. Russell had moved into a parking space from which he could see both exits from the plant. Periodically, the automatic doors would open and disgorge the staff in dribs and drabs. The pedestrians amongst them trudged off down Plasma Glen, heads lowered, shoulders set against the elements. Drivers made a dash for their vehicles, bundled themselves inside, switched on engines, lights, wipers and rumbled off under the roaming, ever-vigilant eyes of the security cameras.

In trim little ankle boots and a leather coat, Dawn picked her way down the steps from the visitors' entrance, handbag pressed to her chest, collar up around her ears. She'd suffered plenty aggravation already but today could well be just the beginning, the first round of inquiries, the initial flap. Tip of the iceberg. Soon Dawn, with her clipped consonants and phenomenal patience, might be deluged with calls from all corners, with panic, outrage, shock horror, real horror, demands for retribution and threats of litigation. The good faith, the trust which had been slowly built up over years between the plant and its customers, between the blood business and the public, what would happen to that? There was no immunity, no state protection. If the plant had screwed up, it was liable. And if he had screwed up?

> *Slip the panels back on, Bobby, turn the dials clockwise and . . . and remove the filter? Remove the filter, Bobby, just lift out the grille from the top and then put your hand in and . . . had he said it? had Bobby done it? . . . if he couldn't remember did that mean he hadn't checked or simply that he couldn't remember? It was quite possible that parts of that particular night had been erased from his memory . . .*

The side door slid open and Morris Morrison ambled out into the night, frowning at the weather. Morris had nothing to worry about. He wasn't an integral link in the plasma chain. Nor were the packers or the delivery boys. They could slope off home and sleep easy. Or drop into their local and enjoy a pint with a clear conscience. Few of the work-force had any information as to the reason for the stoppage but by coffee time that morning everybody had opinions about where the weak link in the chain might be found: needles, phial caps, an air filter. It was maybe a one in ten thousand chance that a bacterium had squeezed through a dozen filters, pulled off a microbial Houdini trick, but it was still a chance. From slush puppy shovellers to computer boys, everybody felt tainted by the knowledge that something had gone wrong and the uncertainty surrounding how it had happened. The safety net had been pulled away from under their feet. Everybody wanted something, somebody to blame.

Everett, his head rotating like a periscope, was at the front door, checking that the coast was clear, that nobody was hanging around the premises, ready to plague him with awkward questions, questions to which he didn't yet have answers. When he was satisfied that nobody was, in fact, lurking in the shadows, he sprinted to his car and was off the site in a matter of seconds. It was hardly surprising that the man was playing hard to get but he couldn't keep up the Greta Garbo routine for ever. Sooner or later, someone would break through Dawn's already stressed-out defences.

Swift and purposeful, Todd strode through the side exit. Where was he off to in such a hurry? On his way to a restorative massage with one of the girls at Fingerplay or Helping Hands? To rendezvous with Germaine Shuck in some city centre wine bar for some full-bodied red and some off-the-record advice?

—Open up, Rusty. Open up, will you?

Muriel was banging on the window of the passenger seat. Russell opened the door and she leapt in, spraying sleet all over him.

—Jeez, I'm glad you're still here. Where have you been all day?

—Here . . . well, I was out for lunch . . .

—Huh! All I got was a pee-break for me and the dog. Those sods in the lab have turned into slave drivers and Big

Boots has been calling up every half-hour looking for results. What does he think we've been doing all day? Tests take time, everybody knows that. And now we've got to stay on late, all night maybe. I can't leave the dog in the car. I asked Dawn if she could take her but she's allergic to dogs. I asked if I could bring her inside the building, I mean, she could sit in the changing rooms. The changing rooms are not so sterile. But now we have this bad blood shit nobody's prepared to put a foot out of step. We have maybe an emergency on our hands and, okay, I don't mind working through the night but I got a dog with nowhere to go, Rusty.

—Out of line, Muriel. A foot out of line . . .

Muriel glared, bit her lip, crushed her arms across her chest and turned away, her hair a glossy black curtain, beaded with sleet. They sat in silence as the windscreen whitened, fleck by fleck.

—I suppose I could take her for the night.

—Could you, really? She likes you, Rusty, you know that. Jeez, that's the best news I've heard all day. I'll go get her. Be right back. Muriel leapt out of the car and slammed the door.

On the top floor of the plant, the labs were still fully lit and might well be all night. Even the hushed, sanctimonious labs, if they had been aware of a rogue virus but hadn't recommended testing for it, even they might find themselves first in the firing line. The car park was now almost empty, the remaining vehicles no doubt belonging to the lab staff who might well be cursing their elevated status now that they were stuck there, lining up culture slides, testing sample after sample in their search for the pathogen, tussling with the Pest Maiden and her innumerable guises. Never mind the bobbing Madonna, the Pest

Maiden should be greeting visitors to the plant; voracious, indiscriminate, invincible, serial killer beyond compare; the Pest Maiden should be floodlit on the landscaped driveway. And constantly monitored.

Muriel had to shove Imelda into the back seat and shut the door quickly so that the dog couldn't fling herself out again.

—She hates other people's cars but if you just keep talking to her all the time, you'll be fine. By the time you get home, she'll need to be fed. Won't eat cheap dog food, by the way, only the good stuff. Pay you back later. Remember to take her out after eating and before you go to bed and maybe you can find something for her to play with, an old slipper or something? I'll come over just as soon as I get out of here, okay? I gotta go. See you later.

Muriel blew the dog a kiss and stomped back to work. Sleet slithered down the windscreen. The dog howled and pawed the glass. As Russell turned into Plasma Glen, his headlights picked out the new night-watchman who was making his way up the hill. As the man raised an arm to shield his eyes from the beam, his creased face bore an unsettling resemblance to Bobby Doyle's, into whose shoes he'd so recently stepped.

THIRTY-TWO

Flesh and Blood

The clock radio blinked every second. The wall socket for the TV made a dry rasping sound, like a fuse or valve about to blow. The fridge clicked and switched on its *I'm working I'm working* whine. In the bathroom, drops of H_2O plus heavy metals and other assorted poisons spattered into the sink. A window rattled and stopped, rattled and stopped. A radiator gurgled. Russell's breath hissed into the sweat-sodden pillow like steam. Imelda, asleep in the basket beside the bed, was chasing dream rabbits or rats. He'd done his best for the dog, starting off with a large can of Supreme Quality Meaty Chunks, purchased from Nice Price. When she heard the dog's name, Mrs Ramasawmy had laughed out loud.

—Very good! That woman is dog!

Sonia and Parveen had come out from behind the counter. They'd patted and cooed. The dog had accepted their fussing with good enough grace. Panjit had murmured that he shouldn't really have dogs in the shop but it was a cold night.

He'd taken her for a walk, fed her, talked to her, let her sit on his feet till they were numb, taken her for another walk, doled out doggy treats at measured intervals, found an old blanket and put it in a basket which Arlene had bought for Boon's but decided was too homespun to complement her fancy food. The basket made a good enough bed and the dog had willingly flopped into it, wriggled around a bit, sighed, yawned and flaked out hours ago. If only he could do the same. It was three-blink thirty-three-blink. The rest of the street was sleeping. Even the patriots across the road – whom he'd not clapped eyes on since the night they battered Lag – were either tucked up under Union Jack sheets or elsewhere . . .

The bed was a shambles, the sheets tangled and damp. He was blazing one minute and shivering the next. Every time he turned over in an attempt to find a position which was comfortable for any length of time, a new pain flared in some hitherto unprotesting part of his body, in addition to the constants; the burning throat, the swollen, parched tongue. Tears brimmed in his eyes, scalding tears. Flu tears. Viral tears. Nothing more than that. Nothing to do with anybody or anything. He'd knackered himself, that was all, squeezed too much into the last couple of days when he should have been taking it easy. He'd knackered himself and allowed the microbes to renew their attack on his already degenerate system. If the body didn't maintain its defences it was asking for trouble, asking to be ambushed.

He should have known better. Yesterday's standing around at Bobby's miserable graveside, followed by the stuffy Lucky Kumquat, the bookshop full of folk expectorating, sending billions of home-grown microbes to go forth and multiply, trailing about in the snow, too much booze, too little sleep, lunch with that Frost woman in a place no doubt rife with high-class, international bacilli, spirilla and cocci. The jumbo jet was a Pest Maiden for the times, roaming the globe, transporting God knows what kind of natural born killers along with its official cargo. Cats and dogs could be put in quarantine but microbes had no problem slipping past an immigration desk.

The blood test – he'd forgotten about the blood test for Morris. Nothing to worry about, Morris had said but that's what doctors always tell you until they come up with a name for the bad news. Nothing to worry about. The condition of his blood hadn't been worrying Russell at all until Morris had offered him that disturbing little platitude. Why did he want another sample? What had shown up in the first one?

He could hear footsteps on the pavement, a woman's footsteps, heels clicking briskly, the footsteps of a woman keen to reach her destination. He lay and listened as they approached, hoping they'd stop, hoping he'd hear the gate creaking open, the doorbell ringing and Muriel yelling through the letter box but they passed by, fading as they continued along the street, leaving him to the blinking alarm and the depressing knowledge that Muriel was still in the labs, filling petri dishes and test tubes, squinting through a microscope at culture slides.

At first, when Arlene had moved out, he'd imagined – and hoped – that every late-night straggler was her. He'd rehearsed all sorts of biting remarks to make in the event of her turning up, contrite, in the small hours, though never had the opportunity to use them. As much as he could use the word of her, he was impressed that Arlene had stuck out camping in Boon's dingy basement for so long. If she and her author had any sense, they'd have sloped off to his hotel. But maybe fucking in the bowels of the old town, bang up against some historical gore was, for her American, one hell of a turn-on. After all, the tourist industry thrived on tales of dungeons and desecrated graves, houses of correction and ill repute, body snatchers and plague pits:

Here is where Burke and Hare drank and hatched plans to bump off their unlucky victims. Here where doctors exchanged cash for carcasses and no questions asked. Here X had his throat cut, here Y was strangled, poisoned, garrotted, bludgeoned, hacked, stabbed, run through, shot, hung, drawn and quartered. These are the bloodstains, this is the weapon, here where the condemned man ate his final meal, here a Styrofoam replica of what he ate. Here the ghosts of dismembered corpses are reputed to have danced the night away, scaring, most recently, a family from Iowa out of their Mid-west wits. Here, plague victims were walled in and left to die; it's said you can hear their cries of protest most clearly on windy nights. Here a fourteen-year-old girl submitted to her breasts being milked by one or more members of the kirk session as proof of her licentiousness, the blackness of her soul. Here, during a time of famine, a starving mother sold her first-born as butcher meat. Here, a lonely crone was alleged to have been seen fornicating with the devil. Here, she was burnt at the stake for the same. Here, a man accused of fornicating with a goat was hanged. The goat was hanged on the same scaffold. This wax tableau illustrates the massacre of a clan, an early example of what would now be called ethnic cleansing. This, Scotland's last queen, on orders from her English rival, is about to have her head chopped off. This, an infamous family of highway robbers who, when pickings became thin, developed a taste for human flesh . . .

Maybe Arlene herself had the makings of a latter-day Pest Maiden, a millennial Typhoid Mary, rising from the depths of Boon's basement in a bloody butcher's apron, offering up her viral specials of the day. Plenty of contemporary killers to choose from but maybe even one or two antique pathogens on special reserve, her nouvelle cuisine tainted by some ancient bacterium preserved in the bricks used to seal up doomed plague victims. If anthrax could survive seven hundred years, God knows what else might be lurking in history's middens as Arlene wined and dined her author on the unbleached calico chairs of Boon's. At a late, intimate dinner for two, Frankie boy might just have bitten off more than he could chew . . .

But what did it matter, what did any of that matter now? He'd got it all wrong anyway. It was made up and the cause of his embarrassment had been, at least in part, his own imagination. If *Eating Passionfruit in Bed* was all he'd got wrong, he had nothing at all to worry about, nothing at all . . .

He is in the computer room. The plant is deserted. It's the middle of the night. It must be, otherwise somebody else would be in there, too, keeping an eye on the close-circuit cameras. There's none of the usual noise from the production line, which begins on the other side of the glass window. Just a hum, a faint low hum, coming from the only screen which isn't turned on.

He is looking for something. He's been sent to look for something, though there is no one around to have sent him. He checks the internal surveillance monitor. All the stages in the downstream processing are normal but the sterile unit isn't coming up on screen. All he's getting is an error message and a flashing red light in the corner of the screen. It is probably a computer fault but he knows he can't quit his search until he can get screen access to the sterile unit. The back-up monitor hums. He switches it on and as he does so, something red begins to seep out of the disk drive, slowly at first, dribbling across the desk, curling over the edge, dripping down, splashing on the floor. He is still in the black section, the unsterilised, germ-filled area of the plant, he is on his own and even though he pulls the plug at the back, blood – he knows by its brightness and viscosity that it's blood – still keeps flowing, spreading over the desk, splattering into pools on the floor. He looks down at his feet. He should have been wearing rubber boots but his feet are bare. He backs off but the blood is now pouring out of the machine. It mustn't touch him. He knows it mustn't touch him but he can't leave the room. The door through which he came in has disappeared. In its place is a door-sized Pirelli pin-up: one topless babe, smeared with black grease, is draped across a car, another identical female wields a hosepipe and squirts foam at the one on the car. The humming has become a rhythmic pumping, like a pulse, a heartbeat. The floor is a red sea and Russell is standing on a chair watching the level inching up towards him. No doors, no windows. The blood on the floor begins to bubble.

—This way, dearie, this way.

It is the Pirelli girls. The poster is no longer a poster but a narrow steel and glass room, like the sterile unit. The car and the hose pipe have vanished. Still covered in filth and foam – and nothing else – the girls now have a microscope to play with. With a sharp steel implement – a cut-throat razor or scalpel — one of the girls is taking skin samples from the other, fitting them into slides and slipping them under the lens.

—Oooh, come close. Come in and see our microbes, darling.

—So clever.

—Sexy.

—Breed like rabbits, rats.

—No, faster, much much faster.

—Against all the odds.

—Infinitely adaptable.

—Limitless possibilities.

A bell begins to ring, an old-fashioned hand-bell. A faint but distinct wail starts up. The girls freeze.

—Unclean, unclean . . .

THIRTY-THREE

Crossing the Water

—Goddamn it, Rusty, you must sleep like the dead.

—Hardly slept at all.

—I rang the bell, knocked on the door, yelled through the letter box . . . so how's my baby?

—I'm not well, not at all well.

—I'm talking about the dog, Rusty.

Imelda trotted down the hall and snuffled against Muriel's trouserleg.

—Did you miss me, did you? I missed you too!

—Are you coming in?

—Sure am. I need to eat. D'you know what we came up with after working all night? Zilch. It's a mystery. A frigging pain too, because until something shows on those petri dishes . . . You look like shit, by the way.

—I told you, I'm sick.

—Everybody's sick. Everybody's gonna die. Here.

Muriel handed him a bag of hot rolls and a packet of freshly-ground coffee.

—Great smell, eh?

—I'll have to take your word for it.

Russell's head felt as if it were full of hot glue. The rest of his body was spongy, distant. He trailed down the hall in Muriel's breezy, exhausting wake, croaking an apology for the mess in the kitchen.

—So, breakfast in bed?

—I should be getting to work.

—Don't be so dumb. You think they want you spitting your bugs about? Call in sick. I'll do it, if you want.

—God, no.

—Nothing in my contract says I can't have breakfast with you. On bed, in bed, or out of it.

—You shouldn't hang about. This virus . . . Morris wants another blood sample. Says it's nothing to worry about but . . .

—So don't worry. No point. Life is a high-risk business.

Imelda had nosed between them and padded back into the hallway where she stood at the door, wiggling her eyebrows plaintively and emitting a pent-up whimper. Bloody dog. After all he'd done for her! All that care and attention and as soon as Muriel turns up, can't wait to see the back of him. No sense of solidarity, loyalty . . .

—The dog needs to pee. Come on then, babylove. Let's go find a lamppost. Back in five minutes.

He filled the kettle, switched it on and retrieved the coffee pot from the back of the cupboard. When Arlene moved out, he'd gone back to cheap, crappy instant which gave him gut ache, but that had been the point: he could then blame Arlene for his declining quality of life. The coffee pot had a fur of blue mould climbing up the inside from being put away wet: a few drops of water was all it took for airborne spores to flourish. He scrubbed it out, washed the dishes, wiped down the work surfaces, noticed, for the first time in weeks, the state of the kitchen floor and phoned in sick. Dawn was so sympathetic that he began to feel a bit better and even found the energy to sweep the crud off the floor and was setting a tray with breakfast things when Muriel and Imelda returned.

They sat on the rumpled bed with the breakfast tray between them. Above the roofs of the tenements, the sky was beginning to lighten. At most there would be six hours of daylight, if the cloud lifted. If not, it might stay half-dark all day. Muriel would go soon. She'd polish off her thickly buttered roll, drain her mug and leave. She had no reason to stay, no reason at all. She'd come for the dog, she'd got the dog and now the two of them could buzz off back to the cottage. He knew he was being selfish and pathetic but he didn't want her to go, to leave him.

—What do people eat for breakfast . . . at home?

—Whatever. Nothing a lot of the time. Depends who you are, same as here. But that country is no longer my home.

—Is this your home?

—Not yet . . . You like that grey on the walls? Too much grey in this country.

—It wasn't my choice.

—Yellow is better.

Muriel poured herself more coffee and began to butter another roll. For someone who'd been working all night she showed no signs of tiredness.

—I called in sick.

—Good. You know how when you're awake when you should be asleep – things look different?

*   *   *

Just as they were approaching the bridge, the sky cleared to a brilliant blue and the low winter sun slashed across the windscreen. Muriel overtook three lorries in a row.

—Does your heart-rate go up when you overtake, Rusty?

—It goes up when you do.

—Huh.

Muriel nudged the pink van into the queue for the toll-booth. The dog, panting cheerfully, edged forward on the back seat, and laid a paw on Russell's shoulder.

—See? She likes you.

Russell scratched the dog behind the ears. When he stopped, she nuzzled into his neck and moaned for more. Muriel rolled down her window and paid the man in the booth.

—You've brought the sun with you, he said.

Muriel flashed him an ear-to-ear grin, put her foot down and roared towards the bridge.

—How d'you think you'll feel?

—I cross the water when I get to it.

—The bridge, Muriel, cross the bridge when you get to it.

—If I cross the bridge, I cross the goddamn water, don't I?

—Okay, Muriel, okay.

The girders glittered. Below the bridge, the firth shone like hammered steel. Russell studied the map to check which turn-off they should take for Burntisland, birthplace of an errant marine biologist. He concentrated on the crazed web of roads which wound through the country, trying not to think about what might have hitched a ride in his arteries, and hoping that Muriel's journey of the blood would turn out well.